THE

GRIMALKIN'S

SECRET

THE

GRIMALKIN'S

SECRET

K.K. WINTERS

Stone Arrow Books
Draper, Utah

Dragon tail image on back cover courtesy Lushpup Images – Geoffrey Dunn Photography, www.lushpupimages.com. Cat drawing at beginning of part one from www.supercoloring.com, used with permission. Dragon art at beginning of part two by Danny Kojima, legendsartmanagement@gmail.com.

First Edition
ISBN: 978-0-9825528-1-0
Library of Congress Control Number: 2012954607

10 9 8 7 6 5 4 3 2 1

To my mother,
whose word games inspired
the idea for this book.

And to my father,
for being my personal editor
and supporter.

Reesk Alphabet

A – ✔   N – ■

B – ♌   O – ⫻

C – ♍   P – ⫽

D – ♎   Q – ‾

E – ⌐   R – ✖

F – ⌐   S – ◆

G – ♑   T – ▲

H – ♒   U – ▼

I – ♓   V – ◆

J – ◖   W – ◀

K – ◗   X – ⫸

L – ●   Y – ⫸

M – ○   Z – ▢

Symbari Alphabet

A – α	N – ν
B – β	O – o
C – χ	P – π
D – δ	Q – θ
E – ε	R – ρ
F – ϕ	S – σ
G – γ	T – τ
H – η	U – υ
I – ι	V – ϖ
J – φ	W – ω
K – κ	X – ξ
L – λ	Y – ψ
M – μ	Z – ζ

Table of Contents

Prologue

PART 1 — THE GRIMALKIN

PART 2 – THE SECRET

Chapter 10
▲ ≋ Γ ▲ ✕ ⫽ ● ●

Chapter 11
♍ ✕ ⬊ ⫽ ▲ ♓ ♍ ○ Γ ◆ ◆ ˅ ♑ Γ ◆

Chapter 12
τ η ε σ ψ μ β α ρ ι

Chapter 13
τ η ε τ α ν ι ω η α

Chapter 14
♍ ˅ ■ ♓ ○ ⫽ ■

Chapter 15
˅ ◂ ˅ ◡ Γ ■ ♓ ■ ♑ ▲ ≋ Γ ♎ ✕ ˅ ♑ ⫽ ■ ◆

Chapter 16
▲ ≋ Γ ◂ ˅ ✕ ♌ Γ ♑ ♓ ■ ◆

Chapter 17
▲ ≋ Γ ⌋ ♓ ■ ˅ ● ♌ ˅ ▲ ▲ ● Γ

Chapter 18
▲ ≋ Γ ◆ Γ ♍ ✕ Γ ▲

Prologue

Even though she was much larger and more powerful than an ordinary cat, Catina felt small compared to the enormous dragons gathered in the cavern around her. Many of them had already been paralyzed by the disease she had conjured. The remainder of the dragon council held a meeting to decide how to deal with the disease. Catina was almost positive that they would leave the caves, then the rest of her group could move in and the mountain would be theirs.

"We are leaving," the red dragon confirmed. "We are the last to move. The sick have been transported. The plague should end soon."

Her plan was working perfectly. The traces of magic the dragons left behind would be more than enough to support the army she had just joined. Catina turned to the red dragon, "I can stay here and try to purify the virus so that the caves will be safe to move back into. The germ doesn't affect me; it was made only for dragons." Catina cringed at her slip of the tongue. The

1

dragons were supposed to believe that the virus was a natural one, not one made just for them.

"Yes, we think the virus was specifically made for dragons too," the yellow dragon said. "It can't be an accident that it only affects us. Most of these viruses attack all magical creatures, not just one species." Luckily, her mistake seemed to strengthen their trust in her so she was safe for now.

The dragons walked to the large hole in the rock wall that looked out across the valley. "Goodbye," the red dragon nodded to Catina. They leapt from the perch one by one and flew off into the night.

Catina waited until they were out of sight then pounced down the mountain, following the winding dirt road to the old hardware store at the edge of town. The manager nodded to her nervously as she trotted past him and down to the basement. She chuckled as she went down the stairs thinking of the manager's face. He was still unused to having magical creatures in his presence. They would wipe his memory when they were done with him. There wouldn't be a problem.

Catina went through a hidden trap door in the basement and down another set of stairs where the beginning of an army was amassed in a wide cavern dug out by magic. She sat at the foot of Zedoc who lounged in a rusty old throne. They would make the fancy throne that he deserved when everyone moved into the dragon's mountain.

"They are all gone," Catina reported. "They won't be coming back either. Can we move now?"

"We must wait," Zedoc answered. "We have to build our cover first. The visitor's center will be done in a week. Everything is assured... except you."

"What?"

"You are unpredictable. You joined us only because you want to find the one who created you and you will be able to find him only when we free all magical beings to come out in the open and rule over humanity."

"So? What difference does my motive make? I'm still helping you," Catina replied in shock.

"You are not completely loyal and we don't need you anymore." Zedoc turned to one of his advisors. "Wipe her."

Prologue

"Wait!" Catina wailed. "I thought memory wiping didn't work on me. I'm magical! You can't have that much power!"

"Yes, we do have that much power. That is why we call ourselves Symbari, the name of the magic that was outlawed so many hundreds of years ago. Goodbye..."

PART 1

THE GRIMALKIN

CHAPTER 1

✕ ♓ ♌ ♌ ♓ ▲

It was midmorning and Kya followed her friends outside. They each had a cup in one hand and were heading to the forest on the edge of Kya's large Wyoming estate. Kya had inherited the estate when her parents died five years earlier in a terrible automobile accident.

"I hope Hemlick fixed the taste of his potion," Eliza said. "Last time we asked him to change the taste, he just changed it from tasting like horse dung and dead leaves to tasting like ear wax and rotten fish." Eliza was twelve years old and lived in Kya's house with her. Her grandfather was Charles, the family butler, and he was the only family Eliza had. After Kya's parents died, Charles had to stay at the house full time to take care of Kya and the estate, so Eliza moved in too.

"Give it up already," Cameron chuckled at Eliza, "Hemlick is never going to make that potion taste good." Cameron was fifteen years old like Kya. His parents were both from Mexico, but when he was born they moved to America for a safer place for Cameron. His father left them when he was three. Ever since then, his mother Maria had been working at the estate as a part-time housekeeper. When Kya's parents died, Charles decided it would be best to have Maria help him run the place so he invited her and Cameron to move in too. His decision was made easier by the fact that Kya, Eliza, and Cameron had been great friends from a very early age.

The trio of kids entered the damp forest and followed a well-worn path next to a small stream. They reached a small pond and dipped their cups into it.

"Well, here we go," Kya said as she took a drink and disappeared from Cameron's and Eliza's view. Then Cameron and Eliza each drank from their cup and an old cottage with a nicely laid rock trail leading to it slowly came into view along with Kya. This was the only way for anyone to get to Hemlick's house.

Hemlick was over two hundred fifty years old because of an enchantment he put on his heart and he was full of knowledge. The man had devoted his entire life to learning everything he could about magic. He had mentored Kya's father in his magical gifts, and now he was mentoring Kya and her companions. After many years of studying, Hemlick had even devised a way to create an enchanted house. The house was made of normal materials but magic held it together. At any time, Hemlick only has to whisper a few words in order to change the dimensions or configuration of the house to suit his needs.

As soon as the taste of the potion wore off, Kya, Cameron and Eliza got up and walked down the rocky trail leading to Hemlick's house. Kya knocked on the door and a voice yelled from inside, "Come in children!"

They opened the door to Hemlick's combination house-laboratory. There were tables everywhere that were covered in chemicals, half-finished experiments, and wacky inventions. They walked in and turned the corner to a room full of junk. Scrap metal, spare parts, and loose wires were scattered all over the floor.

Chapter One

Hemlick was sitting in the center of the room sorting through everything. He was a tall, lanky man with hair that looked like it had been dipped in a mud bath and attacked by an electric mixer. He wore a suit made of at least twenty different materials and a pair of combat boots with rusty buckles. What was most confounding about his appearance were his eyes. They were a bright purple and as big as tennis balls.

"Ah," Hemlick said, "Came for your lesson I suppose?"

"Why else would we come?" Eliza asked sarcastically.

"Eliza!" Kya yelled. Eliza was never very respectful to Hemlick or to any adult for that matter.

"No, no. It's okay. I don't want you to come here for any other reason anyway," Hemlick said.

"You still haven't made your seeing potion taste better," Eliza complained.

"Well, why should I change it for you?!"

Eliza shrugged in response.

"There, you see?! No answer, so I guess you'll just be putting up with that taste for now." Hemlick said getting up and pushing past them into his main lab.

"Do you want to learn something today or not?" Everyone hurried after Hemlick as he proceeded out of the house and into a clearing in the forest.

"Cameron," Hemlick pulled a thick book out of his pocket. "Study Chapter Three and then come get me when you think you have it. We're going to have some fun today."

Cameron took the book and sat on a log at the edge of the clearing. He flipped through the pages and began reading Chapter Three.

Hemlick was already starting with some warm-ups, having Eliza change into animals after he showed her a picture of them. Eliza's mother had been enchanted and Eliza could transform into different creatures whenever she wished. She had to have seen the animals before in order to transform, and she could change into an amazing number of animals.

Kya could use magic and was practicing making acorns disappear and reappear in different locations around the dirt clearing.

Cameron looked up and sighed. He couldn't use magic like Kya and Eliza. He was always studying how to use it and its history but he couldn't use it. *What's the point in knowing all about magic if you can't use it?* he thought.

Cameron looked back at the book. Chapter Three was about pulling energy out of inanimate objects. Everything has energy in it and you can use that energy without using your life energy. This is very important because if you run out of life energy, you die. Cameron learned from this that he had life energy, but he was still depressed that he didn't have the power to draw energy from objects around him or to use the energy for magic.

Cameron finished reading through the chapter right as it started raining. Everyone ran inside as the clouds erupted with lightning and thunder.

"I guess we'll have to do something else then," Hemlick said. "Girls, come over here and we'll do some little things for now. Cameron, you can watch if you like or do whatever you want."

There it is again, Cameron thought. *Why do I even come here? I don't get to do anything.* Cameron sighed and sat down on a bench against the wall. As soon as his behind hit the bench a metal compartment swung out from the wall and banged closed around him.

An eerie glow enveloped the space and Cameron could faintly hear Eliza yelling and banging on the outside walls of the compartment. A metal harness wrapped itself around him and held him in place. He heard an automated voice say, *Analyzing exterior threat*, followed by a muffled thump and then silence from Eliza. *Exterior threat neutralized*, the voice said.

A metal arm descended on Cameron with three needles on it, each a different color: green, blue, and black.

The automated voice continued, *Choose shaping needle.*

Cameron stared at the needles fearfully. Shaping needles? What do the colors mean?

Choose shaping needle.

"Green?" Cameron gulped.

Initializing green shaping needle.

The metal arm jerked foreword and projected the green needle toward him. When it was a foot away Cameron closed his eyes and braced for the worst. He felt a tiny prick.

When Cameron opened his eyes he was on the floor and everything looked very big. The metal cover had retreated back into the wall and Hemlick was standing there looking anxiously down at him. Kya rushed up next to Hemlick and gasped when she saw Cameron. Eliza was there too but not completely. She was sitting on the floor blinking and shaking her head, mumbling something about a giant spring loaded boxing glove that had punched her in the face.

"Oh! You chose the green one!" Hemlick said delightedly and picked Cameron up.

"Why is he a frog?" Eliza asked as she became more aware of her surroundings.

A frog? Cameron thought. *Why would I be a frog? What did that green shot do to me? Can I get myself back? What if I'm like this forever? I'll never be able to swing a bat, or play soccer, or run, or play, or do anything normal again! HEMLICK!!!!!*

Hemlick went on to explain. "Cameron's frog appearance is an effect of the green serum. It is something I've been working on for some time but it's still in the experimental stage. Interestingly, I noticed in early trials that it has a side effect that you girls may have felt. A short energy pulse of the person's human genetic makeup is sent out when they are turned into a

14

frog. I've been meaning to study this side effect more but I've never gotten around to it and – Oh! Look at him! He's turned red! Is that even healthy for a frog?"

And indeed, Cameron the green frog was now the red frog. He was so mad at Hemlick for ruining his entire life that he started swelling up like a puffer fish filled with fury and anguish and was now a bright red. Suddenly, the pressure in Cameron's frog body released all at once spitting a huge glob of frog slime into Hemlick's face.

"Oh my, oh my, oh my! Yuck!" Hemlick peeled the slime off his face and held it up. "Hmmm, I wonder if this could be reused, or maybe added into a translator mechanism... something like..."

Cameron huffed, *Up to Hemlick to turn everything into some wacky science experiment.*

"How do we get him back?!" Kya asked, shaking Hemlick's shoulder to pull him out of his thoughts.

"Oh! What? Yes, yes, um, okay," Hemlick shook his head and hurried away with Cameron still in his hands. When he returned, Cameron was back to normal but none of them had any idea how greatly his transformation would impact them all.

CHAPTER 2

✓ ▲ ▲ ✓ ♍ ☽ ⌐ ♎

All of the magical creatures in their paintings felt the genetic signal that had passed through the museum earlier that day. It was an odd thing to occur, but it didn't mean anything to any of them except, apparently, to Catina. Catina was the cat in the painting called *Grimalkin*. When museum visitors weren't looking at Catina, she fidgeted nervously in her painting and had a look of crazed desperation on her face.

The magical creatures in the other paintings felt sorry for Catina ever since her weird disappearance from her painting for several days eight years earlier. Humans did not notice because the museum was shut down for building maintenance. Ever since then, Catina had never been the same. She couldn't even remember her name.

Now it was night and the museum was closed, and Catina was doing something none of them were supposed to do. She was coming out of her painting. To make matters worse, she was going into other paintings and destroying them from the inside.

Most of the other paintings had been ruined badly by the time Catina entered *The Forest of Pau*. The trees in *The Forest of Pau* listened for anything that would betray the cat hidden in the foliage. Nothing. One of the trees shifted a branch slightly. A low growl erupted from behind a bush. *No!* the tree thought. Green eyes appeared in the shadows and moved steadily toward him.

There was nothing to do except... it was a last resort because it might sap all of their life energy and might not even work. The tree next to him looked over and nodded grimly. He slowly pulled all of his branches above him so they were straight up. The cat froze, wary of whatever this tree was doing.

His leaves stretched up to the sky and then fell to the ground all at once in one big heap. As the other trees and plants saw him do this they all started shaking, their leaves also falling to the ground.

17

A young tree looked out from *The Forest of Pau* to another painting across the hallway. She saw what was left of the sun in the other painting getting brighter and brighter until it was blindingly bright. *Good. The signal is spreading*, she thought. All the other paintings would soon get the word and add their energy to the signal, but it might cost each of them all of their life energy.

The tree that had shed all his leaves saw in his mind's eye all of his brethren in the other picture frames working hard to intensify the signal being sent to Kya. Kya might not recognize the signal, but it was the only option left. She was the only magical being within range of their signal that was both capable and caring enough to help them. The last thing the trees thought before they used all of the power they had gathered to project the signal was: *The Grimalkin will be the end of us all.*

CHAPTER 3

▲ ≋ Γ ♎ ✕ Γ ✔ ○

The sun rose up over the mountains. Rays of light reflected off the lake in front of Kya's house, seeping through the cracks of her window blinds and waking her from a troubling dream. It wasn't unusual for her to have strange dreams but this one seemed more real than normal.

In her dream, she was running through a museum scared of something. The building shook and when she turned around she saw Cameron hanging from the back of his shirt, which was gripped in the jaws of a huge cat. Kya was frozen where she was, as if something were holding her back from helping her friend.

Kya lay on her bed thinking about the dream while examining the long string of gherons running up and down her arm. Gherons were tattoo like symbols that appeared on Kya's body as she progressed in her magical abilities. When she was a baby, her father had enchanted her with the power of ✕ ⌐ ⌐ ♦ ᴗ *Reesk*, or magic. That's when the symbol ᴗ , or "K", appeared on her right palm, a sign of the magic now intertwined in her soul. As she grew and learned new spells, more magic symbols appeared, moving from her palm up onto her arm.

All of a sudden, Cameron burst into the room interrupting Kya's thoughts. "Get dressed," he yelled. "Charles is taking us fishing today. Hurry!" He ran out the door leaving Kya squinting as light from the upstairs hallway streamed into her room.

Kya sighed and pulled herself out of bed, shaking off her worries about the dream and closing her bedroom door. She took out a brush and pulled the tangles out of her long, brown hair. She washed her face and pulled her locks into a loose ponytail.

So we're going fishing, huh, Kya thought. *Something warm should work.*

She pulled a blue sweater out of her closet and orange sweat pants from her dresser. Just as she finished changing, Eliza barged in and jumped onto the bed.

"Kya," she complained. "This stupid jacket doesn't like me again."

"No, it doesn't," Kya observed with a slight frown as she slowly walked over to Eliza. "There we go," Kya said as she zipped up the coat for Eliza.

Kya walked over and opened the window blinds near the foot of her bed. "Looks like a wonderful day to go fishing, but I hope your grandfather brings some snacks on the boat because I'm not going to have time for breakfast."

They walked out of Kya's bedroom and, as Kya was closing the door, she glanced around the room to make sure everything was in its correct place. Her bed was against the far wall in the corner facing the windows to the left of the doorway. Her dresser was against the wall at the head of the bed, and her desk was next to the door of the bathroom. Along the whole wall above the desk hung some of Kya's favorite paintings. If any of Hemlick's magical tests appeared, she would know.

Kya's favorite tests were those that caused complete and total pandemonium because she really got to use her magic. But then there were little tests that bored Kya but Hemlick claimed were necessary, like how well she noticed slight shifts in furniture or other little things, like one of her shoes turning a different color. Hemlick insisted that noticing these small variations in her environment was an essential part of being ready for any possible situation where Kya would have to use her magic.

Right, I still have a magic lesson today, Kya remembered as she tucked the thought away and closed the door. Then she joined everyone excitedly heading out the front door to go fishing.

The speedboat raced along the Sweetwater River, leaving a foamy V in its wake. Eliza leaned over the side, the feel of the wind reminding her of a time when she transformed into a bird.

Kya leaned over the railing in front of Eliza, the rushing wind whipping her ponytail into the younger girl's face. Eliza fell back into the boat spitting the taste of Kya's hair out of her mouth.

"Kya!" she cried. "Pull your hair up!" She gestured at her own hair, "This is why I keep mine short!"

Her hair was indeed short. In fact it was even a bit shorter than Cameron's which, for some reason Eliza could never understand, was always shaggy and raggedy.

I like my hair long, Kya thought as she laughed at Eliza's remark.

Kya helped Eliza up just as Charles slowed the boat to a steady lull and then cut the engine.

"Let's get fishing!" Cameron said, grabbing the fishing poles and handing them out to everyone. Cameron was always excited about fishing because he was so good at it and his mom told him his father had loved fishing.

In the first few minutes Cameron's pole bent over as he yelled, "Fish on!" and in an hour they had caught five fish. Then Cameron's line went taut and he was unable to reel it in. Finally it came free of whatever it was caught on and he pulled a painting up from the depths.

The picture disturbed Kya because she had seen it in her dream the previous night. It was of a very large trout with a marble eye, an exact replica of what she was looking at now.

"Charles," Kya said nervously. "We need to go now." The next part of her dream had been a giant wave that came out of the picture and washed her down the hallway of the museum.

"But we've only caught—," Charles started.

"No. We have to go now," Kya insisted.

Charles knew Kya usually had a good reason for doing and saying things so he pulled his line in. The others quickly reeled their lines in too. In a few short minutes everyone was sitting down with mystified looks on their faces as they sped back down the river. Cameron was the most upset as his fishing had been interrupted and he was never happy about that.

What does this mean? Kya thought frantically. *I'll have to ask Hemlick.* She kept looking behind the boat waiting for the wave to appear. And then it did, sweeping around the bend in the river, rushing toward them.

"Go, go, go!" Kya yelled. The churning soup of mud and water poured down the river toward them.

Everyone was doing their best to help make the boat go faster after seeing the oncoming catastrophe. They threw the cooler and deck chairs overboard, even abandoning the anchor. But no matter how fast they went it wasn't fast enough. The wall of foaming water was gaining on them.

"Good luck you guys," Eliza said, staring up at the bubbling crest of the wave. With one last look at Kya, pleading with her eyes to help the others, Eliza turned into a fish and waited to be washed off the deck. Then everyone looked at Kya for some hope of surviving.

"Wait," Kya said tensing and thinking. *This isn't the first time I've dealt with something like this,* she remembered while trying to calm herself down. *It would be too hard to stop the wave, so a shield would be best.*

"Hamebori," Kya whispered and a rectangular metal compartment rose up from the floor of the boat around them. A cover came together above Kya, Cameron, and Charles. Eliza the fish was still lying on the far side of the deck and was now wishing she'd stayed near the others.

Inside the metal container, the three people clad with life jackets and rubber fishing boots were encased in total darkness. They waited anxiously for the wave to hit and when it did it was deafening. The water crashing on their capsule echoed around in a loud, continuous booming. Cameron covered his ears while Charles braced himself against two opposite sides of the container and began meditating. Even without seeing him, Kya knew this was what Charles was doing. He had spent years practicing it during his CIA training in Cambodia and he had been doing it during tense moments ever since.

The boat flipped upside down, throwing Kya and Cameron against the ceiling of the shield while Charles calmly maintained his position wedged against two of the walls. Even though Cameron couldn't see, his eyes went all speckled with white blotches when his head hit Kya's. The capsule continued to get battered and tossed in every direction until it finally came to a stop in the mud of the riverbed.

Eliza was swimming as fast as she could toward the riverbank. She had no idea what direction it was in and hoped she was going the right way.

I hate these stupid fish eyes! Eliza thought. She thought this because the eyes morphed things that she saw, and she was worried that she'd been swimming in circles. On top of this, the water around her was pretty muddy so Eliza could barely see a few feet in any direction.

As Eliza swam on and on, she wondered how Kya knew the wave was coming. Of course she knew it had something to do with Kya's powers because she had seen the gherons on Kya's arm glowing as the wave came around the bend. But she also knew that Kya did not have the power to see the future.

Finally Eliza noticed a dark patch in the water in front of her and was relieved to discover that she hadn't been swimming in circles. As she swam closer, the shadow molded into a log stuck in the mud of the riverbed, which meant she was close to shore. When she got into the shallower water she began her transformation back into her human form.

Eliza had always hated this part because as the gills were closing up and her lungs began to work, her stomach was never too happy. As she went through the transformation, she lay on the muddy riverbank gasping for breath and then vomited into the river.

When she felt better, Eliza stood up, made sure all of her clothes had rematerialized, and started walking downriver, her boots squelching in the mud.

It had taken Kya long enough to calm her whirling belly and aching body, now she had to find out exactly where Cameron and Charles were in the container so as not to hurt them when dismantling it. Magic was tricky business and being in the wrong place at the wrong time could kill you. With what felt like a broken arm, and no light whatsoever, the only thing she could rely on was sound.

"Cameron?" she whispered.

"Yes?" Cameron whispered back.

"Put your hand out." Kya reached her good arm out and felt Cameron's fingertips. She gratefully grasped his hand. Like a chorus in perfect unison they both whispered, "Charles?"

"What is everyone whispering for?!" Charles asked at a normal volume.

"I... I don't know," Kya said sheepishly, "It just seemed like the right thing to do in such a dark place." Everyone laughed at Kya's answer.

After finding Charles, everyone sat down in a small triangle on what Kya speculated was one of the sides of the container she had created.

Kya tried to recall all of her lessons with Hemlick and all of her previous adventures to figure out how to release them from the container. She had always excelled at building things with magic but the dismantling part was the hardest for her.

Kya closed her eyes and reached out with her mind. This was Kya's favorite part of being enchanted, connecting into the winding current of feelings that flowed through everything. After the stress of what had just happened, Kya thought it was wonderful to open her mind like this.

Just as Kya started thinking of a way to dismantle the container, she felt the tug of another conscience approaching them.

Eliza stumbled through the mud towards the boat lying on its side. *Finally!* she thought, *That boat has taken me forever to find.* "Hello!" Eliza yelled banging on the side of the huge metal container. "Anybody home?" As Eliza thought back on it, maybe she shouldn't have knocked so loudly.

Then a muffled voice came in reply, "Eliza?"

"Yeah!" She'd found them — alive! Even though she was happy to have found her friends, Eliza felt useless now because she had no idea what she was supposed to do to help them get out.

"Kya?" Eliza said, "Do you have any idea how to get yourself out?"

A pause, then some sort of yes. Eliza backed away from the boat, knowing what magic can do. There was a loud pop as the metal container shattered, dumping its passengers into the water. After some splashing around, Cameron, Kya, and Charles were standing on the muddy riverbank shivering.

Eliza perked up at the sound of wailing sirens coming closer. "Hurry!" she said, climbing up the steep hill leading to the road at the top. Everyone else eagerly followed her, teeth chattering all the way.

They got to the top of the hill just as the emergency vehicles raced past them and down the road. The road stretched for miles in both directions. There was no sign of civilization except for an old SUV parked on the side of the road. Kya started toward it and tried to open the door.

"Kya, what are you doing?" Cameron asked.

"Look, we have to get out of here somehow and we can send this car back when we're done with it. It's only ten minutes back to the house, so I'm sure whoever's it is won't mind if we borrow it."

Kya whispered a spell and climbed into the front passenger seat as the engine roared to life. Charles jumped in the driver's seat and adjusted himself to the controls.

Cameron sighed and opened the back door for Eliza. They found some blankets in the back that looked a little dirty but they were better than nothing to warm them up with.

As they drove, Cameron glanced at Kya's reflection in the rearview mirror and noticed she wore a troubling expression. He made a mental note to ask her about it when they got home.

When they got back to the house, Kya whispered a spell and then tapped the SUV. It disappeared and they all headed into the house to take warm showers.

Back at the road near the river, two hunters could not figure out how their missing SUV had suddenly reappeared behind them. They also wondered what kind of thief would leave a thank you note on the front dash.

CHAPTER 4

▪ ▾ ⌐ ♦ ▴ ⱶ ⫽ ■ ♦ ✓ ■ ♎ ✓ ■ ♦ ◂ ⌐ ✕ ♦

It was 8:30 p.m. and Cameron sat in his room pondering the day's fishing trip and the answer Kya had given him on how she knew the wave was coming.

Kya's response was quite frank: a dream. This befuddled Cameron, but Kya would give him no more of an explanation. It seemed as if she, herself, had really no idea how she knew of the wave.

As Cameron sat on the edge of his bed with the setting sun illuminating his room, his attempts to make sense of everything only left him more perplexed. *I doubt Kya is going to give me any more information on this,* he thought. Charles knew quite a bit about magic but Cameron was sure he had never dealt with dreams. And his mom had no expertise in magic or events like these.

Chapter Four

Finally, Cameron put on his sneakers and jacket, having decided what his solution was. He ran downstairs and, on his way out the back door, ran into Eliza.

"Where are you going in such a hurry?" Eliza asked.

"I'm going to ask Hemlick how Kya's dream told her the wave was coming."

Eliza hesitated and then said, "Can I come?"

"Uh... sure," Cameron replied.

A large grin spread across Eliza's face. She was the kind of person who loved to be anywhere that something important was happening.

They hurried across the yard and entered the forest. The sun was dipping below the horizon. They drank from the pond with the seeing potion and walked up to Hemlick's house, knocking on the door.

A loud clattering filled the night as a startled Hemlick dropped his experiment. "Oh now what?! It's not time for a lesson! This night is too busy!" Hemlick complained. A small shutter opened on the door and a bright purple eye looked out at them.

"What do you want?" Hemlick impatiently asked.

"We seek advice," Eliza said in her best mysterious tone.

"Don't make fun of me! Anyway, why should I give you any advice?" the old magician scowled. "You've rarely listened to me before."

"Then I suppose my grandpa wouldn't care if I told him about your exploding spaghetti experiment that almost got us all killed?"

"Oh! That was a fun one, but we don't need him finding out about that now do we? Come in, come in." The shutter on the door slid closed and there was the sound of multiple bolts, locks, and magical traps being removed from the door. Finally the door opened.

"Come on in," Hemlick growled as he hustled them inside, locking the door after them. "Kya! You have visitors!" Hemlick shouted.

Eliza looked at Cameron, wondering if he knew Kya was here. She hoped they wouldn't be in trouble.

"I'm in here," Kya said from around the corner. With Hemlick in the lead they walked toward the room Kya was in, navigating around a huge glass tube that Hemlick was experimenting with. The lights inside the tube flashed on and off as they got closer and exposed a giant man-fish clinging to the side. Eliza jumped back in horror and then slowly side-stepped around the tube at a distance.

They rounded the corner to find Kya lying on a hospital bed with tubes running from suction cups on her head to a huge machine looming behind her.

"What is all this?" Cameron asked.

"It's a long story," Kya said. Eliza took the hint and sat down on a bench in the corner of the room.

"Last night, before we went fishing, I had a dream," Kya continued.

"What does that have to do with anything?" Eliza interrupted.

"Will you let me finish?!"

"Sorry..."

"Cameron, when you pulled up that picture with your fishing pole I got scared because that was part of my dream. And the wave was the next part."

"Oh, that's why you said a dream when I asked how you knew about the wave," Cameron said.

"Exactly, but I don't remember the rest of the dream except for the point where you — never mind. Anyway, I decided to ask Hemlick about the dream and the events that happened and Hemlick said we needed to do some tests."

"Well how long are you planning to stay here?" Cameron asked.

"I don't know," Kya sighed, "I need to stay here until I fall asleep so that Hemlick's machine will pick up my dream. It's supposed to be able to remember it for me so that we won't lose what it's about."

"So you made a machine that documents dreams?" Cameron asked Hemlick.

"Yes, I've been working on it for a few years but I stopped for a while to make an energy sponge that is made of metal and works with—"

"Get back to the dream machine please!" Cameron blurted out.

"Oh! Right. So when Kya told me that her dream came true during your little fishing trip this morning, I pulled the dream machine out of my shed and finished it. As you can see I've attached it to different areas of Kya's head in order to get better reception."

"You talk like it's a TV," Eliza said.

"That's very close to what it is. As soon as Kya has a dream, the machine will play it on this television screen. She should have the dream as soon as she falls asleep."

"Anyway," Kya continued, "Hemlick thinks the paintings in my dream might be the source of the dream itself. And he thinks they might have sent the fish painting and wave in order to convince me that the dream was more than just a dream. We might be able to stop the sequence of events in my dream from occurring if we can find out why the paintings are trying to contact me."

"Contact you?" Eliza said.

"Oh, right! Sorry, on my way here to see Hemlick this afternoon, the dream forced me to sleep — it was like I fainted — and I had the dream again. We think the paintings might be enchanted. The only way to find out for sure is to visit the actual museum in my dream where the paintings are."

"And where is this museum?" Eliza asked.

"That's what we want to find—" Suddenly Kya's head fell back onto the bed and Hemlick's machine started buzzing. Lights started flashing everywhere.

"Here we go," Hemlick said rushing back and forth to different switches on his invention. After a few switches were flipped and buttons pushed, the television screen started humming like a swarm of bees. Cameron backed away from the bed and moved over to where Eliza was.

The red lights on top of the machine turned green. The television screen fluttered to life and panned around a museum hallway. They saw the fish picture from the river. They watched as Kya ran down the hallway and jumped into a painting of a forest. She drew symbols in the dirt that Cameron didn't recognize as Reesk. The letters had just started to glow in the dirt when Hemlick stepped in front of the screen.

"Cameron, I have been informed that you are involved in this dream. From experience I believe it is troublesome to see your future, so I suggest you leave. You too Eliza, I do not trust you to keep a secret." Hemlick said this with such concern and authority that neither Cameron nor Eliza wanted to argue with him. They scrambled to their feet and quickly left the room, casting one glance back at the TV projecting the future.

"Sometimes he just drives me crazy," Eliza said grumpily as they moved to the next room.

"Me too," Cameron said as he sat down on a bench, cautiously looking back for contraptions that might leap out from the wall behind him.

CHAPTER 5
▲ ∾ Γ ○ ▼ ♦ Γ ▼ ○

Kya woke up from the same dream but it was much more intense this time. There was also a name that came to her in her dream: *Dawn*. She popped out of bed and opened her notebook that she used for magic lessons. Hemlick told her to record everything, and her memory was fading fast.

Hemlick hadn't let her see the tape after she woke up in his laboratory the previous night but said, "You will need to discover and solve this dream yourself. It will lead you and your cohorts to discover new strengths about yourselves." Hemlick was often vague and dismissive like that. So, Kya wrote as quickly as she could, recording the word 'Dawn', and continuing to record her dream up until the point where the Shadowed Man lost his knife, and then she couldn't remember any more.

Kya ran downstairs to breakfast. Today was the day they would visit local museums. They had spent all of the previous day researching museums across the world, but none of them seemed to match the museum in the dream.

"Good morning. How are you?" Maria greeted Kya. Maria said everything in such a cheerful way that you never wanted to ignore her or reply in a negative way. She was a fit woman with brown hair, brown eyes, and a heartwarming smile. She could also cook a mean apple pie. Kya thought of her as her second mother.

"I'm great!" Kya replied.

"I made French toast," Maria said in a rising voice looking for Kya's reaction.

"Yes! Thank you Maria!" Kya grabbed a plate and dumped herself into a chair. She slathered her French toast in butter and jam and cut it up with the side of her fork.

The news was on the TV and the anchors were talking about a museum. *What a coincidence*, Kya thought. If something weird had happened at a museum that was making headlines in the news, Kya needed to take a closer look. Maybe this was where the paintings were. Kya held onto her hopes as she asked Maria what the news story was about.

"Some boy disappeared at The Dawn of Painters Museum a few days ago. He was about your age actually. They've had the building locked down ever since and won't let anyone but police in."

Kya ate the last of her French toast. *The Dawn of Painters huh*, she thought. *It can't be a coincidence that the word 'Dawn' came to me last night in my dream. And why would the museum be locked down for several days for a missing boy? Wouldn't the police just collect their evidence and reopen the museum?*

Then she heard Cameron speak from the doorway, "Seems strange they would have the building locked down for so long."

"I agree," Kya replied.

They both looked at Maria who also had a puzzled look on her face. Kya hopped out of her chair, "Well, I guess The Dawn of Painters Museum is our first stop today."

"Sorry miss, this area is in lockdown," the policeman told Kya.

"I think I can help you sir," Kya said ducking under the caution tapes.

"Miss, you can't go in there!" the policeman yelled at Kya as she walked toward the museum.

"Relax," Kya called over her shoulder. "I know what I'm doing."

"Kya!" Cameron screamed, running through the group of policemen standing around and ducking under the caution tape. "What are you doing?!?!"

"Don't worry, they know me."

The policeman made it to Kya before Cameron did and grabbed her arm. "Sorry young lady but I have to ask you to leave!"

"Sergeant Banks, leave her be," a voice said behind the policeman. Sergeant Banks turned to see Chief Nucty.

"Yes sir," Sergeant Banks replied in a respectful voice and let go of Kya.

Chief Nucty turned to Kya, "It's nice to see you again Brunell." Most people didn't refer to Kya by her last name but the Chief always seemed to favor this

44

formal way of addressing people. Chief Nucty was a fit man but his favorite food was donuts and he always joked about his fast metabolism. He had slightly graying hair and a mustache that crawled over his lip. He'd been the local city police chief for twenty years and knew about Kya's magic through her father who had occasionally helped the Chief with his most difficult cases. Kya continued the tradition of sometimes helping the Chief as he was one of the few normal people who knew magic existed.

"Good to see you too, Chief," Kya replied. "What's going on here?"

"I'm sure you've heard the story. A boy disappeared at this museum with no trace and no witnesses of a kidnapping on one of the busiest days of the week."

"Do you have an area?" Kya asked.

"Sort of. We have the place where he was last seen."

"Great." Kya and the Chief led the way into the museum with a breathless Cameron close behind. After getting a nod from the policemen who realized they were with Kya, Eliza and Charles quickly caught up with everyone else.

Cameron wished he had a commanding presence like Kya sometimes did. Kya could get people to do anything, but Cameron had a hard time persuading even his mother to give him ice cream. Cameron felt guilty about being jealous of his friends. He pushed his thoughts aside and followed everyone else into the museum.

"What happened to this painting?" Kya inquired of Chief Nucty.

"That's another part to this mystery. Some of the paintings look like someone came in and painted over them with a mishmash of colors. However, the only paintings apparently being vandalized are the ones in the Unknown Artist section, and the dirty work occurs only at night," Chief Nucty motioned toward the ruined painting on the wall that used to be a meadow with a purple sky filled with orange birds. Now it was a mush of colors and patterns.

"What about the security cameras?" Kya asked.

"They all go blank around the same time every night. On top of that, one of our men went missing while investigating during the video blackout. We haven't released that to the public yet and that is why we've had the building locked down. We really don't know what to do about all of this. I was about to call you just before you showed up."

"Do you have video footage of the boy?"

"Yes, follow me." The Chief walked out of the Unknown Artist section and through a door marked 'Employees Only.' They followed a short hallway into a room with a desk stacked with television screens and a man sitting in front of it.

"Howdy sir, whadda ya' need?" the man spoke in a thick Western accent.

"I need to use your video equipment to give these folks a Top Secret security briefing. Will you please excuse yourself so we can have some privacy?"

"Yes sir." The security man quickly exited the room wondering what could be so important that he couldn't hear it too.

Chief Nucty first filled them in on more of the publicly available details. "The boy is from a Mexican family and his full name is Marco Justino Villanueva

Arroyo. He's thirteen and—" Chief Nucty stopped at Kya's surprised face.

Kya turned to Cameron and asked, "What do you know about your extended family? At least your mother's side of it." Cameron noticed the connection too. Marco's mother's family name was the same as his: Arroyo.

"My mother had three sisters who probably have families of their own by now, but as far as I know, none of them moved to America. They couldn't afford to and the only reason my mom could was because my dad somehow managed to save enough money to pay for it," Cameron said.

"Interesting," Chief Nucty interrupted, "Perhaps this video tape will fill in more of the picture. It comes from one of the museum's security cameras on the day the boy disappeared and I secured it as soon as I saw what was on it."

Chief Nucty pulled the video tape out of the inside pocket of his jacket and plugged it into the side of one of the video machines. The TV screen flickered on and showed a boy walking up to a painting resting on a wooden easel at the front of the Unknown Artist

48

section. The painting was of a cat resting on a cat bed in a red room. The boy traced his hand around the edge of the painting.

"That painting is called *Grimalkin*," Chief Nucty said. In the tape a security guard came into view and yelled at the boy. The boy appeared frightened. As if responding to the guard's attack on the boy, the cat in the painting shifted into a crouch and snarled. The security man backed away and ushered everyone out of the area. The boy stayed and touched the painting again and then he was immediately sucked into the painting. Then the tape went blank.

"I can take care of this," Kya said.

The Chief looked relieved. He'd been around long enough to know certain things were best left to certain people. "Thank you. We convinced the guard who saw the cat move that it must have been a quirk of the lighting in the room and that the sound of the cat's snarl must have been a truck or something from the street outside the museum. I think we still have this situation contained. If there's anything else I can do to help you, just let me know." The Chief turned and walked back through the museum.

Chapter Five

"So," Cameron asked Kya, "Do you know what's going on here?"

"No," Kya said. "But I'm going to find out."

CHAPTER 6

⌐ ˅ ○ ♓ ● ◗

Kya rang the doorbell and knocked three times on the door where the missing boy lived. The door opened and a puffy-eyed woman glared out at them. "¿Qué quieres? ¿No ves que estoy muy preocupada? No necesito ningún niño me molesta!" she yelled at Kya and Eliza in Spanish as she shooed them away with her hand.

Mr. Selsee, the police translator, stepped up from behind Kya and spoke to the woman quietly in Spanish until her eyes showed that she understood. She turned back to Kya and Eliza and beckoned them inside.

They sat down in a living room with Mexican rugs on the walls and beautiful intricate patterns around the room. "Soy la Señora Villanueva Arroyo, Marco es mi hijo," she said with a sob.

"I am Mrs. Villanueva Arroyo, Marco is my son," Mr. Selsee translated.

Referring to Cameron's mom, Kya asked, "Do you know Maria Medina Arroyo?" Mr. Selsee translated that for Marco's mother and her eyes widened, and then she spoke in a barely audible whisper in English, "How can this be?"

Kya was surprised, "You speak English?"

The woman lifted her head and looked deep into Kya's eyes, searching for some sign that Kya could be trusted. She decided she could trust this inquisitive teenager who came asking about her little sister. "Maria is my dearest sister and friend. Have you found her?!"

"I have known her since I was practically a baby and I have lived with her for the past five years. May I ask, what is your first name?"

"Isi. I have not seen my sister since she left Mexico fifteen years ago! Please let me see her!"

"You will," Kya reassured her, barely able to contain her joy at having played a part in a family reunion. She couldn't wait to see Maria's face! "First we need some answers about your missing son if you're okay with that. I'd also like to call in a friend of mine who is waiting in the car. We didn't want to overwhelm you."

"Of course, of course," Isi replied.

Kya stood up and turned to Mr. Selsee, "I guess we won't be needing your translating services anymore. Would you mind waiting in the car while we finish up here?"

Mr. Selsee agreed and followed Kya to the police car parked outside where Cameron was waiting. On the way back up the driveway Kya filled Cameron in on what she had just found out. Kya could see Cameron's joy welling up inside him at the idea of finding more of his family and then his nervousness at not knowing what to expect. When they sat down on the couch across from Isi, Cameron was shaking badly.

"Isi, this is Cameron, Maria's son," Kya gestured toward Cameron. Cameron managed a hopeful smile at Isi and watched her face shift from happiness into complete and utter joy as she swept him into a great big bear hug and dropped tears onto his shoulder. "Pensé que había perdido a ti ya tu madre!" Tears of happiness continued to streak down her cheeks as she released Cameron and sat back down next to him on the couch.

"I am sorry, I am sorry. I was never supposed to see him. I'm not even supposed to be here with him."

"Why not?" Kya asked.

"After Maria married Ricardo and told us about his magic, my parents thought he was practicing some kind of witchcraft and had brainwashed Maria. They were so disappointed and outraged that they banned all contact with Maria and her husband. In childhood, Maria and I had been very close and now I was not allowed to even act like she existed. It was hard for me and eventually I rebelled against my family and moved here to find her, but I could not. I tried so hard, but she lived so quietly that no one knew her. I have been here for two years."

"Thank you for that explanation," Kya said. "You can come with us now if you would like to and we'll take you to Maria." Kya saw the eagerness light up in Isi's eyes like a spark and grow into a roaring inferno as they turned into the driveway of the Brunell estate.

Everyone was silent with anticipation as they went into the kitchen where Maria was scrubbing dishes.

Kya cleared her throat. Maria turned around and saw Isi. First she seemed startled, and then a cold fury entered Maria's eyes that Kya found unfamiliar.

"Maria, this is—"

"I know exactly who this is," Maria spat as she stalked over and slapped Isi in the face.

"Maria!" Kya sputtered.

"No," Isi said. "I deserved that."

"Dang right she did," Maria scowled.

"But why?" Kya asked.

Isi gave a guilty look at Maria who crossed her arms scornfully. "When Maria first got married," Isi began, "She trusted me with her secrets. She told me about Ricardo's power of enchanting and made me swear not to tell anyone. But I told my father thinking that he would be amazed and happy, but instead he was furious. Maria knew it was me who told him and she could never forgive me. I would not either if I were her but I still wish she could." Isi looked at Maria who glared back.

"No te mereces mi amor," Maria said.

"Lo siento!"

"Me has traicionado!"

"Pensé que iba a hacer feliz a todos!"

They continued arguing in Spanish until Cameron covered his ears and screamed, "Enough!" Both women stopped and stared at him. "I finally found a connection to family but you two drag up an old fight and destroy it! You are family!" Cameron yelled, tears streaming down his face. "Family loves each other no matter what!"

"Cameron," Maria tried.

"No! Just stop!" Cameron ran out of the room and stomped up the stairs with Eliza running after him. Kya ran after Cameron too, casting one glance back at the two women hoping they could find the love for each other that they'd had as kids.

"I should not have betrayed you all those years ago," Isi said tearfully. "I am truly sorry. Please, we must try to be family again for Cameron and Marco's sake."

"Apology accepted, but it will take time for me to forgive you," Maria replied. They walked upstairs together to soothe Cameron's fears of losing his newfound family.

After Cameron was reassured that his family still loved each other, he went back to the museum with

Kya, Eliza, and Charles to look for clues on what exactly happened to his cousin Marco.

Maria and Isi stayed at Kya's house after Kya told them that Chief Nucty wanted to keep those going into the museum to just the four of them for now.

When they got to the museum they decided to split up and look for indications of magic. They divided the museum into four parts: 1) Landscape, Monet, and Van Gogh; 2) Portrait, Picasso, and Unknown Artist; 3) Abstract, Matisse, and O'Keeffe; and 4) Klimt, Warhol, and Rembrandt. Each of them took a section and searched all of the paintings and their frames for anything that would indicate an enchantment.

Usually when something is enchanted, the words used to enchant it are discretely hidden somewhere on the object. After going through the Portrait section with no luck, Eliza found eight paintings in the Unknown Artist section with enchantments scrawled in very small symbols on the back of their frames. Five of the paintings in the Unknown Artist section had been turned into a mush of colors, while the other three were in good shape, including *Grimalkin*.

After the search turned up nothing else in the rest of the museum, everyone gathered in the Unknown Artist section. "I should go into the Grimalkin painting and look for Marco," Kya said.

"What about all the police? They think we're just kid detectives helping Chief Nucty with this case in the normal way. They don't know anything about our magic," Eliza said.

"They won't see me."

"But they're everywhere."

"I'll be careful."

"Look," Eliza said, "The security cameras are still running and we don't want anyone else finding out about the magic part of this case."

"But we have to go into the picture sometime," Kya insisted.

"Do we have to do it during the day?" Cameron chimed in.

"No, I guess not," Kya replied, "Maybe we should just work this investigation the regular way during the day and use magic at night when the police are gone. The regular way is just... it's just so boring!"

Kya suggested they all sit down and think. Kya listed off all of the destroyed paintings to herself: *The Forest of Pau, Shale Stories, Lizard Island, Twisted Chasm,* and *Sky Castle. What do they all have in common? All of them are by unknown artists, but they all had the same style of painting so they were probably by the same person. All of them were enchanted and they were all in my dream. What else?!?!*

"Kya? Can we open our eyes now?" Eliza asked as she peeked through her right eyelid. Everyone else was still thinking and meditating but Eliza was becoming impatient.

Kya sighed, "Fine. But only if you keep looking around for clues." Eliza jumped up and tromped off down the hallway. Kya closed her eyes again and went back to thinking.

It's unlikely that a human ruined the paintings because there was no sign of anyone breaking into the museum. No one broke into the museum. Something that was originally here must have done it... the Grimalkin? No... Maybe. Kya opened her eyes. "Eliza!" She got to her feet and ran down the hallway that Eliza had disappeared into. She turned the corner and found

59

Eliza staring with wide eyes at the Grimalkin painting on its wooden pedestal at the entrance to the Unknown Artist section.

Eliza slowly pointed at the bottom left corner of the painting where a pale, scared face could be seen. "Kya... I think I found the security guard," she said in a shaky voice. Kya rushed over and stared at the face, her mind whirling. Cameron came around the corner and peered over Kya's shoulder, "Is that the security guard?"

"Yep," Kya answered, "We'll get him out of there tonight."

"But if he can be seen in there, then why can't we see Marco?" Kya asked, frowning in thought.

"It sounds like we need to think some more," Cameron said.

"No!" Eliza shouted in protest, running down the hallway and hiding behind a tall marble pillar. "I can't stand any more meditating!"

"Fine," Kya called to her. "You can go look up some of Cameron's and Marco's family history on the computer."

"Yes!" Eliza replied as she turned and raced down the hallway and into the security room where the computers were. Kya was glad to have Eliza out of her hair. She could be helpful, but she was the most impatient of all of them. She never wanted to meditate, which helped Kya think, and she never wanted to be cautious, which Kya always told her was important. She would be a handful when she got older. Kya felt sorry for Charles.

But Eliza's stubborn nature had come in handy during some of their other adventures. When they were in Medusa's cavern, Eliza was the only one who hadn't been turned into a statue. The thing is, Medusa doesn't kill you by turning you into stone, she only transports your mind to another realm and your body is turned to stone until your mind is returned. Eliza had refused to look at Medusa's eyes and was the only one stubborn enough to resist their calling.

Kya sat down and began to meditate some more until she could not think of anything else. That's when Eliza came back down the hallway, walking slowly in defeat. "Sorry, I got bored. I couldn't find anything interesting about Cameron's family."

Kya frowned. She shouldn't have expected Eliza to be able to work for a long time anyway. "That's okay,"

Kya decided. "It's getting late; we need to go tell the manager that we need to stay overnight."

"This is so wrong," Cameron said from his stall. "I am never going in the girls' bathroom again."

"I agree," said Charles from another stall.

"Only about an hour to go," Kya said. "Hang on." Right then, snoring could be heard echoing around the bathroom they were hiding in.

"Eliza?" Kya asked. Nothing but more snoring could be heard.

"How does someone sleep in a bathroom?" Kya asked as she peeked over her stall and turned on her flashlight, illuminating a sleeping Eliza in the stall next to her. She had tied her jacket to the posts of the stall that went up to the ceiling. There she was, curled up in her makeshift hammock snoring peacefully.

Kya shook her head, "Eliza, Eliza, Eliza..."

Cameron flicked his flashlight on, "Can we get out of here yet?"

"No, but soon," Kya replied.

Cameron's sigh resonated around the cramped restroom. No one but Eliza was comfortable. This reminded Kya of a time when they were playing hide-and-go-seek as little kids. Cameron was it. Kya, Eliza, and Maria were all hiding. Kya clearly remembered climbing into a little box that rested on the hard wooden flooring of one of the rooms in her house. She had to curl up tightly in order to fit into the box and had cramped up after only fifteen minutes.

Maria was found first and then Kya, but Eliza was entirely missing. They had searched high and low for her but no one could seem to find her. After a while they gave up, hoping she would come out on her own. When she didn't, they really got worried.

Eventually they found her on one of the shelves in the linen closet, snugly sleeping in a pile of bed sheets. She was completely hidden by the shelf above her and the sheets around her. Those were the good old days, when they didn't know enough about magic to get into real trouble.

Kya checked her watch: 10:30 pm. They had told the manager that they needed to stay overnight, but he wasn't happy with the idea and said no. Instead of bothering Chief Nucty who was busy with other cases, Kya decided it was easier for them to just hide in the bathroom.

Kya reminded everyone of the plan, "The watchman should be done with his first round at eleven and then he goes up to the control room. Last night the security cameras went out from 11:30 to midnight. Let's find out if something is happening at that time tonight that is worth seeing."

"What do you think is destroying the paintings?" Cameron asked nervously.

"The Grimalkin," Kya replied.

"What?"

"It's just a hunch for now," Kya said. "What I really wonder is why all of this started now? The Grimalkin painting has been at this museum for twelve years. Why would it all of a sudden start attacking other paintings and people now? Unless..." Kya went silent in thought. Cameron waited for her to continue but when she didn't he prompted her, "Unless what?"

"Cameron, what did Hemlick say that green needle did other than turn you into a frog?"

"Um... I don't know, something about, like, transmitting a genetic signal out or something like that."

"Exactly. These pictures may have picked up your genetic signal. The boy disappeared the same day you were turned into a frog, so maybe the two are connected in some way. But why would your genetic signal make the Grimalkin act up? I can't make sense of that."

"Almost eleven o'clock," Cameron reported.

"Okay, Charles do you think the Grimalkin acted out by coincidence, or do you think the broadcast of Cameron's genetic signal is connected?" Kya asked.

There was no answer.

"Charles?"

Cameron looked over his stall and saw the old man lying in a makeshift hammock of his own and staring straight at him. "Aaaah!!!" Cameron yelled as he jumped back, hitting his head on the opposite side of his stall. Cameron clenched his teeth and rubbed his throbbing head as he slowly peeked back over the stall. Charles hadn't moved, in fact, he hadn't even blinked.

It must run in the family, Cameron thought, referring to the hammocks Eliza and her grandfather were now lying in.

"He's sleeping," Cameron said. "In a hammock. With his eyes wide open!"

"Oh," Kya said sheepishly, "I guess no one ever told you. He does that — sleeps with his eyes open. Another trait he picked up in the military."

"Right, well, that's creepy," Cameron said and tried to shake the image out of his head.

"11:15," Kya reported.

Good, Cameron thought, even though he was slightly nervous. *A cat that destroys paintings. That was new. Usually magical adventures involved revenge, madness, and power. But a cat? How bad could a cat be?*

It was 11:30. The painting *Dreams* stared nervously into the darkness of the museum. A growl erupted from the blackness. The surviving paintings had rehearsed what to do if she showed up again and all of the colors of all the paintings rose to the top of their canvases like a rain cloud about to burst, and then the colors dropped as they sent another signal to Kya.

Cameron could feel something watching him. He didn't know what it was, but it was something. The darkness and the fact that a cat might be prowling the building made the feeling scarier. But things got much worse when Kya passed out.

They were just walking out of the bathroom when Kya started to wobble, then completely fell to the ground as if in a coma. Everyone panicked for a second, but after Charles explained it had to be the dream again, they lifted her onto a bench and left her there.

Kya had suggested they look at the Grimalkin painting so that's where they started. The cat was not in the painting and that scared the bejeebers out of all of them. They walked with caution after that.

They were in the main hallway when they heard the growling. When the cat emerged from the shadows, it was much bigger than it was in its painting. It was about half as tall as the twenty foot high glass ceiling over the Unknown Artist section and as muscular as a bodybuilder. The huge cat advanced toward them menacingly. Cameron could feel its stare penetrating deep into his soul.

Just when he thought it was going to eat them all, Kya stepped up from behind them with a new gheron glowing on her arm.

"Not today cat," Kya said defiantly. The cat's eyes became clouded as it fell asleep on the floor and then disappeared in a cloud of dust.

"Did you kill it?" Eliza asked, trembling.

"No," Kya said. "Just returned it to its painting."

"What do we do now? Why do you have a new gheron on your—" Eliza started to ask.

"Leave," Kya interrupted, only answering Eliza's first question, "Whatever you want to say, save it for later. We have to get out of here."

CHAPTER 7

○ ⫽ ✕ ⌐ ♍ ● ▾ ⌐ ◆

Eliza went to her room right as she got home. The curious part of her brain begged to stay awake and try to figure out how Kya saved them. Kya had been lost in thought all the way home and would not answer any questions. Eliza also wondered why Kya insisted they leave. There seemed like a million other questions running through Eliza's mind that she wanted answers to, but the rest of her body just wouldn't allow it and she fell asleep as soon as she laid down on her bed and her head hit the pillow.

The next morning Kya woke everyone up at eight o'clock to go back to the museum. "Why do you want to go back there?" Eliza complained. "You were in such a big rush to leave last night."

"I know, but Marco's disappearance still isn't solved," Kya replied.

"Ugh," Eliza groaned tiredly as she rubbed her eyes.

They went straight to the museum after breakfast. They inspected every painting again. They had finished looking at all of them when Kya and Cameron went back to one of a dirt clearing surrounded with trees. "I remember this one," Kya said. "It's from my dream."

"The one where you drew in the dirt?" Cameron asked.

"Yep."

"Then why don't you draw in it now?"

"I don't know what to draw. Those symbols I drew in the dream... I haven't learned them yet."

"Then how did you draw them in the dream?"

"I don't know but—" Kya stopped and the gherons on her arm started glowing and shimmering. Her eyes shone green with such intensity that Cameron thought they would burst. Three new symbols appeared but not on Kya's arm this time. One looked like a "w" with a line on top, another was an "n" with the bottom elongated, and the third was like a cursive "x", and they made a half circle around Kya's left eye. Kya's glowing eyes dimmed and she collapsed on the ground, panting.

"Are you okay?" Cameron asked urgently.

"Yeah," Kya gasped. "I'm never supposed to get gherons that fast."

"Well, what is it? It doesn't look like anything from Reesk," Cameron said pointing to the gherons.

"It's ancient," Kya replied. "Some old magic alphabet that I shouldn't have discovered but the paintings are making me aware of."

"'The paintings are making me,' gee that sounds funny," Cameron said.

"I know, I know, but I'm serious okay? The symbols I wrote in the dream, I know them now. Somehow. The thing is, I only know those, no more no less."

"So go write them in the dirt!"

"Didn't we decide I shouldn't go into paintings during the day?"

"Well, I'm not spending another night in the girls' bathroom!" Cameron insisted.

Kya was uneasy. Her dream ended with Cameron in danger, in the Grimalkin's mouth. If she did everything she did in the dream, then that's where Cameron would end up. If she refused to write in the picture she would have to tell Cameron why. Hemlick

71

had convinced her it was bad for someone to know his or her future even if it's only one possible future.

They looked around to make sure no one else would see them. Cameron stood on a chair and pointed the security camera in the corner away from the painting. Kya took a deep breath and jumped straight into the painting of the trees with the dirt clearing. She was enveloped into a three-sided room with black walls and a miniature sun shining light on the clearing she was standing in. Shadows were cast on the ground by the trees around her. She knelt in the dirt and began to draw the characters as they popped into her head: σηαδοωκνιφε.

The shadows around the clearing began to group together in a shadowy ball above Kya and out dropped a knife. It was about as big as her hand with a black handle and intricate carvings on the blade.

Kya held onto the knife and jumped out of the painting. Immediately Cameron asked her what the knife was.

"It's a key... to the Shadowed Man," Kya replied and pulled Cameron down the corridor until they came to a painting with an outline of where the knife used to be. The painting was called *Shadowed Man*.

Cameron's eyes widened, "You stole the knife from this painting?" he asked.

"Sort of, but I'm giving it back," Kya assured him.

The future should not be changed, Kya reminded herself. *Time will find some way to make that cat capture Cameron. Maybe I save him after that. Until then I must reenact my dream.*

Kya turned to the painting and began to read off the Reesk symbols carved into the blade of the knife. When she finished, the shadows in the painting stirred like a boiling pot of water. A face appeared on the black mesh, pushing itself outward, trying desperately to escape the painting.

"Give it back!" the face screamed at them in a voice that made Cameron think of a vampire looking for the right moment to pounce.

"Woh! Hang on a minute," Kya said. "You want your knife back? I need to know a few things first."

"Fine," the face answered in a remorseful voice as it settled back into the painting.

"What does the Grimalkin do to the paintings?" Kya asked.

The Shadowed Man quietly explained, "She goes into them and destroys them from the inside."

"Why is she doing that?"

"She is a cat," the Shadowed Man said as if the information he was about to give was completely obvious. "Cats are animals and they need family. She was going into the other paintings and wreaking havoc because she was in a desperate search for family." He said this last sentence staring directly at Cameron. Kya followed the Shadowed Man's gaze and looked at Cameron as if he were a specimen of interest.

"The Grimalkin wants Cameron because he is family?" Kya asked in a puzzled voice.

"That is correct," the Shadowed Man replied. "Now give me my knife back."

"This is nonsense. Give him his knife back and let's get out of here," Cameron insisted.

Kya shrugged and placed the knife back in the Shadowed Man's painting then followed Cameron down the hallway.

"What do we need to do now?" Cameron asked.

"We need to go into the ruined paintings," Kya replied.

They were about to turn the corner when the Shadowed Man's voice stopped them. "Kya," he said in an ominous voice. "The Symbari have found you." With that Kya fell to the ground in a deep slumber and all of the lights in the museum went out.

CHAPTER 8

⅃ ∥ ▾ ■ Ω

Kya woke up with Eliza sitting next to her and three flashlights set in a circle around them pointing up. Outside of their little circle of light it was pitch black, with not even a glow from the security lights.

"Oh goody, you're awake," Eliza said, shuffling a deck of cards. "I've had to play cards all by myself."

"Oh no, the horror," Kya said sarcastically. She sat up and looked around. The glow from the flashlights lit up a few paintings that seemed to be staring at her. She slowly stood up and grabbed a flashlight. From the style of the paintings she figured she was in the Portrait section which meant the main lobby was down the hallway to her left.

"Where are Cameron and Charles?" Kya asked turning back to Eliza.

"They went off looking for that cat. Is that dangerous?"

"YES!!!" Kya replied in disbelief.

"I told them that but they didn't believe me," Eliza said defensively.

"I've got to go find them before—"

"Before what? Come on, quit hiding things. You've got to go find Cameron and Charles before what?"

There's Eliza's stubbornness again, Kya thought, "Even I don't know how the story ends, but it's bad to know any of your future so I can't tell you."

"Fine. Whatever," Eliza sat down and started shuffling the cards again. Kya sat down next to Eliza and put her arm around her.

"Hey," Kya soothed. "Some things are better kept a secret, and I think you know that by now." Eliza knew what Kya was referring to. On one of their previous adventures, Eliza looked into a tree's soul and has been connected to that tree ever since. It was very hard for her to keep it a secret from her friends at school, just like it was hard to keep it a secret that she could transform into animals. It was even harder with the tree though because every tree she walked by whispered to her and it drove her crazy not to tell anyone else about it. But in the end, she knew it was best to keep it a secret.

Magic was always better off when no one knew you had it. There would be a small amount of time right after everyone found out where they would be amazed, but they would then start to resent not being able to have this power themselves. Often people would send everything they had to destroy or shun those who could use magic.

After Eliza connected herself with the tree, she even wanted it to be kept a secret from Hemlick because he was always telling her not to be foolish. If he knew what had happened — even if it wasn't harmful — he would have given Eliza the biggest lecture of her life and probably have disconnected her from the tree. She loved that tree so much that they all kept it a secret and covered for her when she went to the tree.

Kya and Eliza sat in silence until Cameron and Charles came running down the hallway.

"Are you guys insane?" Kya screamed at them.

"No but we're in big trouble," Charles replied.

"How so?" Kya crossed her arms. A loud banging echoed down the hallway and she could hear the roaring of the Grimalkin.

"We set a trap and it's in there but it won't hold for long. How do we stop it?"

Kya was already gathering the flashlights. "We can think about that later. Right now we need to think about our safety. Let's go!" They ran down the hallway and turned the corner right as the Grimalkin snapped out of the trap.

"Split up! Confuse her!" Kya yelled and turned into the Abstract section. Out of the corner of her eye she saw Charles and Eliza run into the main lobby and Cameron sprint into the Landscape section. Kya turned her attention ahead of her and dove under a bench made of wooden planks. She laid completely still and wanted desperately to hold her breath because it seemed like it could be heard from a mile away.

She peered out from under the wooden bench and watched the Grimalkin lope by her and into the main lobby where Charles and Eliza went.

"Don't hurt the cat," a voice next to Kya whispered. Kya jumped and hit her head on the top of the bench.

A dark skinned boy was sitting on the floor next to the bench who looked kind of like Cameron.

"Marco?" Kya whispered.

"That's me," the boy whispered back proudly.

"You're alive!"

"Yeah, the cat threw me out. I guess I wasn't who she wanted. It's kind of weird that she didn't let the security guard go though, maybe she didn't trust him not to tell anyone that she is enchanted."

"Why haven't you told anyone that you're okay?" Kya asked.

"Well, the cat showed me a lot of stuff that I didn't understand but I did understand that she's not evil. She doesn't want to hurt anybody. The reason I haven't come out of the museum yet is because I haven't thought of a cover story. If I told the truth and they believed me they would destroy the cat, and if they didn't believe me they'd probably try to put me in an insane asylum."

Kya relaxed for a moment. She had found Marco! He was safe. But then she remembered Eliza and her grandfather were in the main lobby where the Grimalkin was headed. Kya crawled out from under the bench, "Stay here, I'll be back, I have to go help my friends." She jumped to her feet and skidded around the corner in time to see Charles thrown across the main lobby into the wall and go limp. She ran to him, unnoticed by the Grimalkin, and checked his breathing. He was still alive.

The Grimalkin swiped at Eliza and sent her flying into the glass doors which shattered at the impact.

"No!" Kya screamed. Her whole dream was unfolding and there was nothing she could do about it. She wished it would stop. She wished she could cast a spell and it would all be over. She wished everything could be fixed with magic, just like she believed when she was little. She wanted to be able to fix this with words but that wasn't how it worked.

The Grimalkin swung her head around to stare at Kya. She growled and prodded right past her, disappearing around the corner.

Why didn't she attack me? Kya wondered. She leaned around the corner and saw the Grimalkin sniffing the air. *What is it looking for? Cameron?* Kya was absorbed in her own thoughts when a voice spoke up next to her, making her jump for the second time that night.

"What do you think we should do now?" Charles asked, slumped on the floor next to Kya. He had crawled over to her and chuckled at her surprised face.

"I'm not sure," Kya replied, "Maybe we should try to shut down the enchantment, but then again I have a feeling the cat doesn't want to kill us. If she did, she would have killed us all by now. I don't know why, she just seems to have a gentleness in her eyes like it's all just a game to her. And one of the paintings told me that she just wants Cameron because he's family, whatever that means."

"Well then let's — oww!" Charles tried to get up but a splitting pain burst through his head and he sat back down.

"It's okay," Kya said. "You stay here and I'll figure something out." Eliza had crawled out of the glass wreckage and come up beside Kya and Charles.

"We need to get you to the doctor," Eliza said to her grandfather. Eliza was pretty beat up herself. She had scratches on her face and arms and she had just pulled a small piece of glass out of her elbow.

"I'll be fine, we can do that later," Charles said grimacing through the pain but still unable to get up. "The Grimalkin is on the loose and that's what we need to worry about right now."

Eliza didn't want to argue so she changed the subject, "Cameron told me what happened at the Shadowed Man painting. What did the Shadowed Man mean when he said 'The Symbari have found you'?"

"I'm not quite sure about that," Kya replied. "There are a lot of things I can't make sense of." There was silence for a while until Eliza had an idea.

"Kya, why don't you go into the pillaged paintings like you suggested before? Maybe it could help us figure something out about the way the Grimalkin attacks or something."

"Good point!" Kya quickly moved over to a ruined painting called *Sky Castle*. As soon as she jumped in, there was chaos. In the painting the walls were white with bars of color roped across the room. There was a constant buzzing sound with blurps and blips mixed in. Kya ran through the maze of colored bars to a large claw scrape on the back wall. She placed her hand on it and muttered, "Siriloso quidosti." The scratch slowly molded together until the wall looked brand new and the sounds stopped. Kya looked around and noticed a whimpering bird curled up on a twisted branch.

"It's okay," Kya said and reached out to the bird. "I'm here to help." The bird crawled into Kya's hand and Kya gave it a gentle hug. The bird was about the size of Kya's palm and was a bright blue with orange tipped wings. "Can you talk?"

"Yes," the bird's voice was small and scared.

"I think I can help you get your home back," Kya said as she set the bird down and thought about what kind of spell to use. She put her hand on where the scratch used to be and plunged a mental needle of medicine into the wall. The colors started reshaping themselves and before long the whole painting was back to normal.

"Wow!" The bird exclaimed as he looked around at his restored home and flew up to the ceiling, singing happily. Kya was glad he was happy and left the rest of the animals to come out of their hiding places. She leapt out of the painting and walked down the hallway to another ruined painting, *Twisted Chasm*.

She jumped in and again there was chaos but a different kind. This time it was scary echoes and screams that reflected off the walls. Kya could barely make out the winding gulley that originally ran through the middle of the painting. It had several cracks through it, and in different places those cracks lead to black nothingness. Kya carefully perched on the edge of a cliff near one of the cracks and did the same thing she did to the Sky Castle painting. The entire painting healed up and friendly echoes came up from the canyon below. A couple hiking in the lower area lit up with joy in their painted spotlight as they emerged from their hidden cave.

Kya knelt down and picked up a small rock, "You can send this with my energy in it to the other paintings to restore them." She put some of her energy into the rock and threw it down to the couple. Then she heard a sound that was definitely not an echo.

"Thank you!" the coupled called, but Kya wasn't listening. She was already out of the painting and running as fast as she could in the direction of the screams.

CHAPTER 9

♌ ♓ ♑ ♦ ▾ ✕ ⁄⁄ ✕ ♓ ♦ ⌐

C ameron lay face up on the museum bench as the
Grimalkin towered over him. One of her heavy
paws rested on his chest, restricting his breathing.

I'm dead, Cameron thought. *All I did was
accompany Kya to this stupid museum and now I'm
going to get eaten by a giant cat.*

"Cameron!" he heard Kya scream when she skidded
around the corner. Kya started to run toward Cameron
and began to mutter a spell, but a deep growl erupted
in the Grimalkin's throat that stopped Kya in her
tracks. The cat laid one of her claws across Cameron's
neck as a warning. Given the crazed look in the
Grimalkin's eyes, Kya did not want to call what she was
pretty sure was just a bluff. Even if the cat did not *want*
to kill Cameron, she might *unintentionally* kill him
while trying to make a point.

"I found the cat," Cameron called feebly from his unfortunate position.

Kya gave him a sarcastic look, "Really?"

Cameron gulped, "How are Charles and Eliza?" he asked casually, trying to sound less scared than he actually was.

"Fine," Kya answered his question while scooting closer. If she could just get close enough to Cameron, she might be able to construct a protective shield around him. Sadly, the female cat noticed and placed her other front paw on Cameron's chest.

The breath spilled out of Cameron's lungs as the extra weight pushed him harder against the bench. He tried to hold it in, but in the end a loud groan escaped his lips. He felt his chest compress and a loud crack resounded from his torso. His breast bone erupted in blazing pain and he yelled out again. Kya winced and stepped back to where she had been. Unbeknownst to both of them the Grimalkin winced too at Cameron's cry.

The cat did not take her paws off Cameron, but instead sat back on her haunches, wrapped her claws around Cameron's chest and over his shoulders, and lifted him off the bench. Cameron grasped at the bench legs frantically as he was pulled toward the cat. The wood of the bench legs had splintered from the weight of the Grimalkin on top of him, leaving his hand scraped and bleeding. Again Kya tried to step forward, but again the Grimalkin noticed and growled.

A thundering crash rang from the hallway behind Kya and everyone, including the Grimalkin, turned to look. A huge lion with flame red fur came bounding around the doorway right behind Kya, letting loose an earsplitting roar. It would have crushed Kya had she not dove out of the way just in time. A huge furry paw landed right where Kya had been only a second before, leaving claw marks on the hard marble floor.

"Eliza," Kya whispered to herself. "I'll make you be more careful next time."

The Grimalkin didn't hesitate for a second. It dropped Cameron like a sack of potatoes, hissed and then lunged at the lion, sending both of them sprawling on the floor in a hissing, roaring, frenzy of fur. They slammed into the wall with such force that the building shook and several paintings were knocked off the wall, some of them splintering as they hit the floor. Kya made a mental note to repair all of the damage later.

The lion began to bubble and swell, changing into Eliza for a moment and then boiling into a pelican that soared over the cat. It grew until its wings brushed the walls and it was bigger than a great white shark. The Grimalkin was mad that her prey had gotten away and hissed in fury.

Cameron wanted to get up and help but his chest was in too much pain and he doubted he'd have the strength to even sit. His head felt woozy and his hands throbbed with bleeding wounds.

The Grimalkin jumped at the pelican and managed to just reach its tail, pulling out some of the bird's tail feathers. The pelican squawked and shrunk in order to evade the Grimalkin who was jumping and clawing at the pelican as it flew overhead.

Meanwhile, Kya knelt beside Cameron examining his injuries. In addition to his bleeding hands from trying to grasp the bench legs, he had a big gash on his right knee which could be seen through a rip in his pants. But her biggest worry was the crack she had heard when the Grimalkin pushed on Cameron's chest and the gaping wound in his left shoulder that the Grimalkin clawed when she lifted him off the bench.

Kya put her hands on Cameron's chest and started to heal that wound first. She could see the relief in Cameron's face as his pain subsided. She was about to start on his shoulder when she noticed Cameron's eyes getting wider and wider with fear while staring at something behind Kya.

"What?" Kya asked as she turned around, and then she too was wide-eyed and open-mouthed.

The pelican had grown again and was swooping down toward them, trying to get to them before the Grimalkin did. It opened its huge beak and Kya realized what was happening. She jumped over Cameron and held onto his left arm to protect the wound on his left shoulder.

"Eliza!!" Kya screamed but her yell was swallowed up into the pelican's mouth as it scooped them into its beak pouch. Kya added this to her mental list of things Eliza would never hear the end of.

As Cameron and Kya were bounced about in the pelican's beak, the Grimalkin stopped momentarily to spit out the feathers she had pulled from another lucky strike on the pelican's tail. She coughed up the final feather and looked up at the bird, an intense glare in her eye, almost seeming like madness, and crouched low to the ground with her rear end high in the air. Then she shot forward and clenched her jaws into the pelican's right wing.

Kya and Cameron were buffeted with an ear-splitting shriek inside the pelican's mouth. They were jostled around as the Grimalkin tore the pelican out of the air and both kids gasped for air as the pelican burped up some very odd smelling gasses. The stench inside of the bird's mouth smelled like rotten fish. Kya never knew that Eliza's transformations included stomach contents. She would have to ask Hemlick about that when she got home, *if* she got home.

The Grimalkin released the bird's wing and it fell to the floor. The Grimalkin kept ripping at the wing until the pelican went limp and began to bubble again.

"Get out!" Kya yelled. She grabbed Cameron under the arm and he cried out in pain.

"Wrong shoulder!" he cried.

"Sorry!" Kya switched to Cameron's right arm. The beak began to change into lips and the whole area began to shrink. They stumbled to the wall of teeth that started to protrude out of the flesh. Before the transformation they were sitting in the bird's pouch with plenty of head room, but now they were barely able to crawl out of the half-bird half-human mouth.

Just as the bird transformed itself back into Eliza, Cameron got his foot out of the shrinking mouth.

The Grimalkin bolted forward and knocked Cameron aside like a bull while Kya ran in the other direction. The Grimalkin turned and jumped toward Kya who screamed as the Grimalkin's bared teeth were coming down on her.

"No!" Cameron screamed as he started sprinting toward Kya who, at the same time, raised her glowing arm and yelled: "Ghandiza!" The world stopped with the Grimalkin frozen in midair. Cameron was still bolting at Kya. He tackled her with his good arm and they lay on the floor breathing heavily.

"Cameron, the spell—," Kya started to say, but she was too late. The Grimalkin crashed to the floor and slid across the room on its marble surface. When she came to stop, the Grimalkin snarled and quickly wheeled around to face Kya and Cameron. Kya and

Cameron stood up slowly and stared at the Grimalkin's menacing expression thirty feet away. Kya grasped Cameron's hand which was cold with sweat.

"Run," Cameron whispered. And they did, running around the corner to the Cubism exhibit. On the far wall was a knight painted by someone named Henriches Vuatima.

"Bien kanzidin... Bien kanzidin... Oh blast it all!" Kya stamped her foot in frustration. The Grimalkin was rounding the corner now. They could hear its claws scraping on the floor.

"What are you doing?" Cameron asked.

"I forgot the word for 'knight'!"

"What?!?!?!?!?!"

"Ummm... I'll use 'warrior' instead," Kya said. "Bien kanzidin mydon kei!" Kya finished with the gherons up her arm and around her eye glowing. The knight climbed out of his frame and bowed to Kya.

The Grimalkin burst into the room and bared her fangs. The knight from the painting frowned and jumped back into his picture.

"Argh!" Kya shouted. "I should have said *brave* warrior!" Kya pointed her hand at another painting, this time of a jungle with red ants all over the leaves. "Bien kanzidin mydon fan de." Ants flooded out of the picture along with a few vines and mosquitoes. The insects swarmed up the Grimalkin's legs but she was too big to cover completely. The Grimalkin shook them off and jumped at Cameron sending both fifteen-year-olds scurrying into the Monet section of the museum.

They turned around expecting the Grimalkin to be coming in for the kill, but she was gone. They backed up against the wall watching the exhibit beyond, expecting the Grimalkin to come pouncing around the corner at any moment. All of a sudden, the wall behind them rumbled and then exploded as the Grimalkin burst through the wall, sending Kya and Cameron against the opposite wall.

Kya's vision burst with red dots, clouding her sight. Blood dripped down the side of her face and she felt the pain of a large splinter in her left calf. Kya struggled to her feet and froze when she saw the Grimalkin holding Cameron triumphantly in her teeth by the back of his shirt. The cat turned and lumbered off down the hallway with Cameron in her mouth.

Just like in my dream, Kya observed. The thought unsettled her.

Kya fell back to the ground and pulled the shard of wood out of her calf. "Minzen siel," she weakly muttered and her calf stitched itself back together until all that was left was a scar. She did the same with her head then lay down to consider her options.

I have to go after Cameron. The Grimalkin may not want to kill us, but she's doing a great job of maiming us. I don't know how much more of this we can take. Kya decided her best option was to follow the Grimalkin like a spy and from there work to get Cameron back.

As she began to leave in the direction the Grimalkin left, Kya heard a groan from an adjacent hallway. Kya followed the groan down the hallway leading back to the Landscape exhibit.

She turned the corner and gasped, seeing Eliza lying on one of the benches across the room. After the Grimalkin had chased Kya and Cameron into the Cubism exhibit, and later the Monet section, she had almost forgotten about Eliza.

Eliza groaned again, this time rolling her legs off the bench and settling onto her knees on the floor.

"Eliza wait!" Kya called running toward her. Kya slid on her knees the last few feet and skidded to a stop in front of Eliza. She pressed her hand against Eliza's ripped up arm and started to heal it.

"No," Eliza groaned pushing Kya's hand away. "You need to save your energy and I need to go to Grandpa. I will be fine."

Kya got up with a serious face. She could tell Eliza would be okay even though she was in a lot of pain. "You're right. I never knew someone so small could ever be so brave and wise." Eliza let out a weak laugh and began crawling in the direction of Charles.

Charles dabbed his bleeding head with a handkerchief for the umpteenth time and tried to stand up again. His head still throbbed from being thrown against the wall by the Grimalkin but he had to get to Eliza. If he lost her he would be devastated. If she lost him she would have no one.

Eliza can fend for herself for a while until I can get to her, Charles convinced himself. If he died rushing too much to get to her, he wouldn't be of any help at all.

Charles walked slowly down the hallway using the wall for support. By the time he turned the corner he was huffing and puffing for breath, but his breath completely left him when he saw the heap of clothes a few yards away. He ignored his own pain and hobbled over to Eliza who must have passed out on her way to him.

"Eliza," Charles shook her shoulder. There was no answer. "Eliza!" he shook her with more urgency, fearing she was dead. This time she opened her eyes and groaned. "If you think someone's dead but you're not absolutely sure, don't help them get there. That really hurt my arm."

Now Charles noticed the gash in Eliza's arm that he had been shaking and felt bad for not seeing it before. "Come on," Charles said. "Let's get you up."

They slowly helped each other walk back into the lobby and then sat down on the floor with their backs against the wall. Eliza promptly passed out from exhaustion, leaning her head against Charles' shoulder.

Cameron hung in the Grimalkin's mouth with spit dripping down his back. He was frozen in fear but at the same time wondered why the Grimalkin was being so gentle with him.

Cameron could see the Grimalkin painting up ahead as the cat carried him down the hallway. With Cameron in her mouth, the Grimalkin jumped into the painting and set Cameron down on the cat bed. Cameron observed the space of the painting with fearful eyes. The walls were all a deep red and the only furniture was the cat bed he was lying on.

Suddenly, Cameron's mind was flooded with memories of a man he somehow recognized as his father. He now knew why the Grimalkin had taken him. He puzzled over this for a moment and then he noticed the security guard that had gone missing, cowering in the corner.

"You can leave," Cameron whispered to him, "But you must promise not to tell anyone what you saw. Promise?" The guard nodded his head in fear. "Just jump out of the picture," Cameron told him. The guard gave him a grateful smile then rolled out of the picture frame and ran down the hallway.

After Kya watched Eliza leave for her grandfather, she set off for the Grimalkin painting.

Maybe I can save the guard at the same time I save Cameron, Kya thought as she rounded the corner.

She made it to the hallway leading to where the Grimalkin painting was kept. Halfway to the picture she stopped and took a breath. Thinking that now was the time she must save Cameron, Kya began sprinting down the hallway toward the Grimalkin painting. "Quidquid neidyoso," Kya whispered as she dove full speed into the painting.

Inside the painting, Kya rolled to a crouch. She was astonished at what she saw. There the Grimalkin sat, licking Cameron like crazy! It was like she was grooming his hair. The Grimalkin was so relaxed she must have thought that no one could get inside her painting.

Cameron wriggled out from the huge cat's paws and jumped at Kya, wrapping his arms around her so tight she almost couldn't breathe. Kya couldn't believe it. *What is wrong with you?!?!* she thought. *I didn't want to be seen. You'll just get us both in trouble now that the Grimalkin knows I'm here.*

"Don't let go of me," Cameron whispered in Kya's ear. "It's like she thinks I'm her kitten and if I'm close to you she won't hurt you. I think she might even accept you. I know it has looked like she wanted to hurt or kill us, but all she really wanted was to get to me and you guys were in her way."

Again, Kya was in disbelief. Why would the cat want Cameron? What did this mean? But no matter her questions, Kya whispered back to Cameron, "I trust you," and held onto him as tight as she could.

The Grimalkin swept them up and sniffed Kya experimentally. Cameron felt Kya stiffen for a moment then relax as the Grimalkin licked her back. Then, most unexpectedly, Kya began to laugh.

I can't believe this! Kya thought. *We came here tonight to destroy this cat and stop her from pillaging the paintings, but look at what she really wanted! It's so funny that the cat just wanted Cameron after we thought she wanted to kill us. I guess the guard probably just saw her when she was out of her painting one night and she didn't want anyone else to know of her magic so she took him into the painting. But wait... where is the guard now? And why did the Grimalkin want Cameron in the first place? How could he be 'family' to her?* Kya let go of Cameron and gently stroked the cat's nose.

Cameron started to laugh too. Kya pushed her troubling thoughts aside and they laughed and laughed and laughed in relief.

Then Cameron started to explain his knowledge, "Somehow, I know all of the Grimalkin's memories. It turns out her painter and enchanter was my dad. "My dad used to visit her in the museum a lot, sometimes even joining her in her painting when there wasn't anyone around to see him go into it. He would momentarily disable the security cameras in the area to make sure it was never caught on video."

101

"Hold on," Kya interrupted, "If your dad was an enchanter that would make you an enchanter too."

Cameron was a little surprised, "Wouldn't I have known before now if I could enchant?"

"Not necessarily, sometimes you never know you can do something until you really try," Kya replied.

Cameron smiled a little, but inside he was jumping for joy. *I'm an enchanter! I'm no different than Kya and Eliza!* Cameron always felt like the third wheel just slowing them down because they could both use magic and he couldn't. Now they were equals!

Cameron decided to hold his enthusiasm for later and went on with his explanation, "About ten years ago my dad stopped coming to the museum and the Grimalkin lost the scent of his life energy. For over two years she waited for him to come back. There are some blank spots in her memory, but about eight years ago she concluded that my dad must have died, so she gave up hope.

"Then Hemlick's frog serum made her aware of me, including the scent of my dad's genes. The result was a renewed search for my dad thinking he must still be alive somewhere.

"She took Marco that afternoon when he was looking at her because she was in such a frenzy and he smelled somewhat similar to me. It was a mistake though because Marco and I only share genes through our mothers. She let Marco go after she realized he wasn't the right person. What I do wonder though is why Marco wouldn't have shown himself by now. Why is he still missing?"

"I found Marco during the fight," Kya interrupted. She went on to explain why Marco didn't want to tell the police until he had a cover story. Cameron was a little surprised that Marco wouldn't seek help, but it seemed noble to sacrifice his own comfort to take the time to make sure the Grimalkin's enchanted nature was never discovered.

Cameron continued, "Anyway, the reason the Grimalkin pillaged the other paintings was because she thought maybe my dad was somehow trapped in one of his own paintings and was sending out a genetic signal for help. The pillaging was all just the desperate actions of a very lonely cat looking for the only person who had ever cared about her.

"When we all got to the museum, she came after me because I had the scent of my dad. She's figured out that I'm not my dad, but she knows I'm very closely related and that seems to be good enough for her.

"The security guard was just in the wrong place at the wrong time. He and the Grimalkin ran into each other when he was on his night patrol and she was out of her painting. She felt she had to hold onto him so he wouldn't tell anyone about her magic. I let the guard go just before you showed up on the promise that he wouldn't tell anyone. He was so scared that I don't think we'll have any problems with him spilling the beans. Who would believe him anyway?"

Kya nodded. It all made sense. They both slid off the Grimalkin's belly and sat down next to her, leaning their backs against the cat's warm fur, feeling the vibrations of her purring. They were both silent as they remembered fighting what they thought was a killer cat.

Eliza was sitting on the floor in the main lobby next to Charles, wondering where Cameron and Kya had gone. Her wondering increased when they came around the corner laughing.

The two friends came to a stop in front of Eliza and her grandfather. Seeing Eliza's puzzled expression Kya and Cameron both started cracking up again.

"Did the Grimalkin mess with your head or something?" Eliza asked.

"No," Kya laughed. "Cameron's dad painted and enchanted the Grimalkin so Cameron is connected just a bit. From that he—"

"I learned that all the Grimalkin really wanted was family, and that was me," Cameron finished.

Eliza couldn't believe it. She liked to act smooth and clever all the time, but her jaw dropped when she heard that after everything they had been through, the cat wasn't really trying to kill them after all but was just looking for Cameron. "I'm tired," Eliza said as she turned her dropped jaw into a yawn, still trying to cover her astonishment.

"I think we're all tired," Charles said.

Kya laughed. She helped Eliza to her feet and helped keep her steady because of her wounds. Cameron did the same for Charles with his good arm.

"Oh wait! Stay right here, I'll be back in a minute," Kya said. She gently set Eliza back down and ran back into the depths of the museum.

"I wonder what she's up to," Cameron said. They all sat back down, as exhausted as they come, until Kya came back down the hallway with Marco walking behind her.

"Look who I found," Kya said as she presented Marco with an exaggerated sweep of her hand, proudly announcing that the case was closed.

The group slowly hobbled off into the parking lot and drove back to Kya's house. Everyone got a good night's sleep after a tearful reunion between Marco and Isi and a large dinner in celebration of a family reunited.

PART 2

THE SECRET

CHAPTER 10

▲ ⁓ ⌐ ▲ ✕ ⫽ ● ●

"Ten thousand dollars," a man at the back of the auditorium said.

"Twelve thousand," Kya countered. They were bidding for possession of the Grimalkin painting. Kya was determined their new friend would come home with them.

Although Cameron could have visited the Grimalkin in the museum like his dad did, they all knew the Grimalkin would prefer to be closer to Cameron. Kya had asked Chief Nucty if he could arrange for them to get the painting, but the best the Chief could do without saying anything about magic was to get the museum to auction the painting off.

This was fine with Kya since she had lots of money that her parents had left her. Kya normally did not spend her money extravagantly, but this was important.

"Thirteen thousand," the man bid again.

"Seventeen thousand," Kya replied confidently.

The man nervously licked his lips, "Seventeen thousand five hundred."

"Eighteen thousand five hundred," Kya announced.

"Pass," the man sighed. The hall erupted with cheers as Kya marched up to the podium and took the Grimalkin painting from its easel. She held it high above her head grinning.

When Kya walked back into the crowd, she was overwhelmed by people wanting to shake her hand and congratulate her. Many of the adults were amazed at how young she was.

Kya tucked the Grimalkin painting under her arm and pushed her way through the crowd. "Let's get out of here!" she called to her friends. "I'm being mobbed!" Charles put his hand firmly on Kya's shoulder and led her out of the room.

"That was cool how you outbid that guy for the Grimalkin," Eliza said in admiration of Kya.

"I guess," Kya said, then turning to Cameron, "If it's okay with you I think we should put the Grimalkin in my gallery since all the paintings there are enchanted and it's close to where your room is."

"Yes, I think that's fine," Cameron replied and then pondered for a moment, "I don't think we should call her Grimalkin anymore. The name just doesn't seem to fit."

"What about Suzy?" Kya suggested.

"That's a silly name!" Eliza scoffed.

"Fine then, what do you suggest?" Kya shot back.

"Calley," Eliza said with confidence.

Kya responded with a snort.

"Okay then. Cameron, you decide. Apparently Kya doesn't think any good names are cool," Eliza said.

"Lone," Cameron decided. "Because she was all alone for a long time after my dad died."

"He died?" Eliza asked, surprised.

"Yeah, I got a summary of the Grimalkin's, er, I mean Lone's, memory when I got close to her. As best she can remember, she lost the scent of my dad's life energy around eight years ago and the only real explanation for that is that he passed away."

"I'm sorry...," Eliza said in a subdued voice, not sure what else to say.

"That's okay," Cameron replied, "I really didn't know him well since he left when I was three. I don't have much of him to miss."

The group was silent for a while, remembering their ordeal only five days before. Charles broke the silence, "Now, Maria has been busy making a fantastic lunch and I think we better go enjoy it."

"Splendid idea," Kya said like a princess, adding a British accent to her voice that made everyone laugh. They pushed open the big wooden double doors of the auction building and stepped out onto 24th Street where their minivan was parked at the curb.

This was another example of Kya living humbly. If she wanted she could have a limo, but no, the old family minivan was good enough for her.

"I guess everything will be normal then," Cameron said as they got into the van and drove off. "Well, except for my new powers!"

Kya smiled, "I know what you mean. It's super exciting when you first learn you can do magic. In the beginning, you'll use magic all the time just for fun because it's so amazing! The bad news is other magical things will be attracted to you and it's your responsibility to deal with them."

Cameron groaned, "I don't want to be special anymore."

Charles slammed on the brakes as a troll ran in front of the van. They could tell it was a troll by his dwarf-like stature and oversized shoes to accommodate the large claws that all trolls have for feet.

"See what I mean?!" Kya yelled. "Come on. Let's go see what that troll is up to."

The gang got out of the van and left Charles to park it, running off in the direction of the troll. They followed the troll to one of the biggest shopping malls in town. *Why would he go here?* Kya wondered. There was nothing in this mall except expensive stores and cheap vendors, nothing that a troll would be interested in. Trolls usually went after things like enchanted rocks, tasty fungi and sewer water, but he wouldn't find any of those in here.

The troll suddenly ducked into an alley near the glass doors leading into the mall. They watched as the troll flickered into a tall old man in a deep purple cloak and then casually strolled out. The trim of the cloak

113

was dull gray and covered with symbols. One of them Kya recognized as ϕ from the symbols she drew in the dirt at the museum.

"Symbari," a voice whispered in Kya's head and an explosion tore through her mind. Kya screamed and fell back into a parked car.

"What is it?" Eliza asked. Eliza felt just the way she did at the side of the river not knowing how to help Kya lower the shield she had created: utterly helpless. She wished she'd paid more attention to all of Hemlick's classes so she could have some idea of what to do.

"Ahhhh!" Cameron screamed and grabbed his head. "Get it out!"

"Get what out?" Eliza screamed back. What was going on? What was in their heads? Suddenly Eliza was very afraid. Kya's mind was very strong from all of the lessons she had gotten from Hemlick, and so was Cameron's from many of the same lessons even though he did not yet know how to exercise his powers very well. If this force could break them, what could it do to her?

She slowly turned, shaking, to face the old man who had now approached them. He stared down at Eliza from only a few feet away. She stared stubbornly into his eyes, "Let my friends go."

"How about no," the man answered in a high pitched and mocking voice.

"What have you done to them?"

"They must join us," the man said sternly. "They are very strong."

"Let them go!" Eliza lunged at the old man as hard as she could but he grabbed and twisted her arm with one hand and grabbed her hair with his other hand.

"Why are you doing this?" Eliza managed through her tears.

"I am not trying to hurt them."

"It sure doesn't look that way to me," Eliza said as she elbowed the man in the stomach and slipped out of his grasp. Eliza tried to transform into a gorilla but the power drained from her. "What are you doing?!?!"

"You cannot fight the Symbari. We will always prevail. Your friends are strong and they will be of good use to us. You are too young and undisciplined; we have no need for you. Leave us alone child."

115

"Never!" Eliza swung her fist at the old man's face but he caught it. She kicked and hit him but nothing seemed to faze him.

"You are troublesome," the old man said. His fingernails punctured Eliza's skin and she fell to the ground in a sleeping heap. The man walked over to the slumped bodies of Kya and Cameron. He whispered a few words and vanished into thin air with both of Eliza's friends.

CHAPTER 11

Ꮽ ✕ ⬱ ⧸⧸ ⬆ ⴺ Ꮽ ◯ Γ ◗◗ ⌄ ♈ Γ ◗

*Y*ou can't let them go. They will destroy everything. You must stop them. Your friends must escape before they can be transferred. Do not submit. Don't let them hurt my family... Eliza awoke in her own bed. Charles sat next to her reading the morning paper.

"Where's Kya and Cameron?" Eliza asked. She hated the thought that they could really be gone. Maybe it was a dream. It *had* to be a dream.

"I'm not sure, we can't find them anywhere," Charles confirmed Eliza's worst fears. She fell back onto the bed, tears rolling down her cheeks.

"No, no, no, no. I have to..." Eliza sat up. *You can't let them go,* she remembered from her dream. "Grandpa, I need Hemlick."

"Relax, you had some sort of poisoning. You need to lie down."

They will destroy everything. "No, I have to find Hemlick." Eliza stood up and raced to the door. Her head spun and her vision blurred.

You must stop them. Eliza stumbled down the stairs and ran into Maria. "You're up!" Maria exclaimed. Eliza pushed past her desperately, "I have to get to Hemlick. I have to help them."

Your friends must escape before they can be transferred. "Eliza!" Maria called as Eliza ran down the hallway. "You should be resting!"

Do not submit. "I can't stop! I won't! I have to go. I have to keep going!" Eliza screamed at the top of her lungs.

Don't let them hurt my family... Eliza stopped at the back door. *My family?* "Lone," Eliza whispered as she backed against the wall and slid to the floor. "I need Lone."

Charles ran around the corner and let out a big sigh when he saw Eliza, "What's going on with you?"

"I couldn't stop him. He stopped me from changing. How could he do that?" Eliza looked up at Charles, "Grandpa, I just want them back."

"We all do," Charles said in agreement.

"I will get them back no matter what," Eliza said, "And Lone's going to help me." Eliza stood up and ran upstairs into the gallery. She rushed over to Lone's painting where the cat lay in misery. She was withered and dirty like a chewed up animal carcass. Eliza gasped when she saw her. "Lone... what has happened to you?"

My family is gone. The Symbari army is gathering. You have to help, Lone projected her thoughts to Eliza.

"Can you help me?" Eliza asked Lone.

The Symbari are restraining everything. They can keep you from transforming. I cannot come out of my painting because I will not join them.

"Where are they?"

Lone hissed as she tried to answer the question. *They found me. They are in a cold place. Deep and dark... No! They are taking me. No! No!* Lone hissed again and began to disappear from the painting.

"Lone!" Eliza cried but she was already gone. Eliza sat on the floor half pondering Lone's answer and half despairing over her disappearance. Charles came in after a while and sat next to her. "So I suppose you're going to want to do something about this?"

"Yes, of course. Why haven't you?" Eliza accused her grandfather.

"I caught up with you kids at the mall just in time to see the old man take Kya and Cameron. I have informed Hemlick. He is working on it as hard as he can. We've been watching you in case the old man or someone else comes back for you."

"I doubt that will happen," Eliza mumbled. "The old man said I was too troublesome... Is that true?"

"Noooo," Charles said slowly. "You just... uh... have your own way of doing things sometimes."

Eliza laughed, "You're a terrible liar!" The moment passed and Eliza went back to feeling horrible. Charles left to get a progress report from Hemlick and Eliza stayed in the gallery to think. Now she finally understood why Kya liked it here so much. She could see how the quiet and tranquility of the gallery could really help a person think. Without Kya around, Eliza decided to try meditating by herself and to her surprise she got more voices in her head.

120

Help them. When they are free they can dominate. Gather the Great Ones. Help my brethren before it is too late. Eliza thought about every word from the new message and carefully dissected each sentence to get to its core meaning.

Help them. This could mean Cameron and Kya or maybe it referred to other prisoners that the Symbari had captured.

When they are free they can dominate. Whoever they are talking about is obviously powerful if they can dominate the force that overcame Kya and Cameron. But then why isn't this force already free if they are that powerful? Eliza needed to free someone or something so that they could destroy the Symbari.

Gather the Great Ones. The Great Ones? Who could they be? Hemlick might know and that could give her a place to start. Maybe they are the ones that need to be freed.

Help my brethren before it is too late. Whoever was sending the message, more of his or her kind needed help.

Eliza noticed that the message was very clear, so the sender must be very close. She got up and walked through the rest of the gallery. It wasn't very big, just four marble walls zigzagging through the room with paintings hanging on every wall.

At the third wall was a painting of a dragon sitting atop a mountain watching a glowing sunset. It was a very majestic picture and it was the only one Eliza could think of that could have something to do with the "Great Ones." After all, dragons are great, right?

Eliza paused before she went up to the painting. She needed to be careful here. The Symbari had just taken Lone from her painting when Eliza talked with her so maybe the Symbari had the power to eavesdrop on their conversations. But she had to risk talking to the old dragon to try to get information.

Eliza stroked the picture frame and whispered softly to the dragon, "Do not give any exact answers or the Symbari may take you. Tell me in riddles. Where can I find the Great Ones?"

The dragon looked at her with mournful eyes and then gazed back at the beautiful horizon in his painting. In a voice scarred with wisdom and loss he replied, "People walk where they were so they dare not be free. The deceivers throw their lines out but the dragons catch not their lure. Near their caverns that have been taken by those who pretend to plea, they find themselves bound by a terrible sickness for which they must find a cure."

Eliza left the picture and walked back to Lone's empty painting. *Who are the deceivers who throw their lines out? Do they fish or something?* Eliza had to remind herself not to take the riddle's words so literally. It was a riddle after all; it wasn't supposed to tell you exactly what it meant. She thought through each line carefully as she had the other message.

People walk where they were so they dare not be free. So somebody kicked the dragons out of their home and humans are there now. Maybe humans kicked the dragons out. Meanies. Maybe it was unintentional. Maybe humans didn't know the dragons were there. Eliza tried to find a way to defend her species but a small thought was gnawing at her in the back of her mind. Maybe humans did it on purpose. Maybe they knew the dragons were there and got rid of them because they wanted the place for themselves. But then again, maybe humans didn't do it; maybe the Symbari did.

She moved on to the next sentence. *The deceivers throw their lines out but the dragons catch not their lure.* Somebody tried to catch the dragons. The dragons wouldn't bite. Eliza guessed those people were the Symbari.

Near their caverns that have been taken by those who pretend to plea. Who would pretend to plea? A charity group that takes the money for themselves? Maybe they act homeless and helpless when they're actually really rich and well off.

They find themselves bound by a terrible sickness for which they must find a cure. So the dragons would fight back but an illness is disabling them and killing them off. Of course! If they're so great they wouldn't let themselves be kicked out of their home. They must have been weakened by some mysterious plague and couldn't fight whoever took their caverns.

"Thank you old dragon dude," Eliza whispered as she got back up and started walking around the gallery again thinking about every other painting that might be related. After half an hour she got sick of it all and began yelling at every painting. As she turned away from The Spectrum painting, the Woman of the

124

Spectrum whispered, "You couldn't possibly *drive* there you dimwitted human."

Eliza spun around but the woman had faded back into the colorful designs and patterns of *The Spectrum*. Was this another clue? She ran downstairs into the garage and looked all over the minivan. She noticed two stickers on the back. One was for the car's registration and the other was for the company that made it: Durkher Auto Center, Alpnach, Switzerland.

"Switzerland?" Eliza wondered. She didn't want to put him in danger, but she had to question the old dragon further. She couldn't afford to waste time going to the wrong place in her quest to find Kya and Cameron.

Eliza went back up to the gallery and whispered to the old dragon again, hoping the Symbari weren't listening at that moment, "Nod your head, yes or no: Switzerland?"

The old dragon moved his head up and down. That answered that question, but Switzerland was still a big country.

"Near the auto factory?"

The old dragon nodded again. Then in a sudden and exaggerated voice he shouted, "You cannot fight the Symbari! They will defeat you! The Symbari are the most powerful force on Earth!"

Eliza was alarmed at the old dragon's outburst and backed away thinking he might be some kind of double agent for the Symbari.

"I'm glad that worked," the old dragon sighed. He told Eliza that his outburst was just to fool the Symbari. "You must hurry," he said, "Three days until they start the war. You must stop them. Find the dragons known as the Great Ones in the mountain near the auto factory. They will help you." Eliza nodded and took off running to find Charles.

CHAPTER 12
τηεσψμβαρι

"How can they be stronger than the Progenitor?" Fourdin said in his raspy snakelike voice nodding toward Kya and Cameron.

"The oracle said, 'They are stronger than the Progenitor' so it must be true," Jagdin replied. His gelatin body shivered sending a disgusting squelching sound echoing down the dark, stone hallway.

"If that's true then we are doomed," Fourdin seemed so devastated Kya almost wanted to let them win. She'd been listening to the guards talk for hours while they thought she and Cameron were sleeping. Cameron actually was sleeping but Kya was still awake.

They appeared to be in a small prison cell in a mountain. At least Kya assumed they were in a mountain. It was cold and dark with rough stone walls so it seemed a logical conclusion. The worst part of their situation was that the bars of the cell they were in somehow restricted their magic.

"The Progenitor is the strongest force of magic in the world," Fourdin said smugly. "They can't be stronger than him. They're just children."

"The oracle said this would happen. She's always right," Jagdin shivered again. Kya had to stop herself from plugging her ears against the disgusting sound.

"You know what the council is planning on doing with these two?" Fourdin asked. Kya froze at his sentence and then pretended to roll around in her sleep toward where Cameron lay. As soon as the guards weren't looking she clamped a hand over his mouth and he woke up. She pointed at the guards and motioned for him to listen.

"Not really," Jagdin replied. "All I heard was something about the Taniwha." Fourdin listened intently as his long metallic tail scraped back and forth along the hard rock floor.

"The shape-changer child is digging for secrets from her paintings. I can feel it. She is so irritating," Fourdin hissed. Fourdin had been helping the Symbari for a longer time than Jagdin and had more powers than

128

him. "Continue with what you overheard from the council."

"Well, they kept talking about how the beast would deal with these kids after they were of no use to us and I figured they meant the beastly shape-changer in the cave at the end of the river, the one called Taniwha."

Jagdin continued to go on and on about the Taniwha until they were interrupted by a gruff voice yelling up the stairs, "Get em movin' ya dimwits! Progenitor wants ta see em!" Both guards scrambled for their keys and then stopped at the same time thinking the other was going to get their key first. Then they both grabbed their keys at the same time and tried to shove them in the lock at the same time.

"Let me do it!" Fourdin hissed.

"I got it first snake face!" Jagdin spat back.

"No, I got it!" Fourdin tried to shove Jagdin out of the way but got stuck on his slime.

"Get off me!" Jagdin shoved back with a slimy hand to Fourdin's forehead. They were bashing at each other over and over, bickering and making so much noise that neither of them heard the head jailor screaming at them from the lower level.

Kya used the noise to her advantage and whispered to Cameron, "As soon as they get the door open we should be able to use some of our magic. I'm going to use the handcuffs on their belts to cuff them together. I can make a spell for that. You need to use the enchantments that you picked up from Hemlick over the years to make sure they end up in our cell. I know you don't have a lot of practice yet but just try your best. Do you think you can you do that?" Kya whispered everything as quick as she could because the fight was ending quickly.

"I think so," Cameron replied. He was really nervous. He'd only used magic a few times since learning he could enchant. Now their lives depended on him doing it well. His palms were sweaty as he ran through the enchantments in his head making sure he wouldn't mess up.

Fourdin and Jagdin were still going at it in their petty dispute until Fourdin had had enough and walloped Jagdin in the face, barking at him about respecting his elders. Jagdin reeled backwards and fell unconscious on the ground. Fourdin reached for his keys and unlocked the cell door. As soon as the door

130

opened Kya whispered a spell that made the handcuffs fly from Fourdin's belt. They wrapped themselves around his hands and clicked shut. Fourdin's eyes widened in disbelief.

Cameron knew that was his cue. He closed his eyes, concentrating on the enchantment he'd remembered. Fourdin yelled out as the cell door smacked him in the butt and he went flying into the cell that held Kya and Cameron. Since Jagdin was unconscious from Fourdin's blow, Cameron had to think of some other way to get him into the cell. He closed his eyes again and concentrated. The cell bars bent outward grabbing Jagdin by the leg and tossing him into the cell.

Kya stood up, brushing her hands against her pants saying cheerfully, "That was easier than I thought it would be. You did great! Let's go." They headed toward the stairs but ran smack into the head jailor who had come up to deal with the fighting guards. Kya slowly looked up the tall guard's buff body until she got to his face which was twisted with anger. He roared, showing his black teeth and smothering Kya in onion breath. The ogre threw Kya across the tiny room into the rock wall and then turned his attention to Cameron.

Cameron backed up into the cell bars trying to draw the guard closer. The guard took the bait and moved closer to Cameron. The guard smiled again, believing that he had won. He pulled his fist back to deliver the fatal blow to Cameron when the cell bars lashed out and smacked him across the face. He was dazed. Cameron concentrated harder and the bars smacked the ogre again and again and again until he dropped to the floor with a blissful but unconscious smile, still displaying his rotten teeth.

Cameron stepped over the ogre's body and ran to Kya who was trying not to cry from the wound on the back of her head. "It's okay," Cameron soothed. "You can heal it can't you?"

"I don't know," Kya sobbed. "I'm not sure I can think straight enough."

Cameron crouched and put his hand on her shoulder. "What was Hemlick starting to teach you before we ended up here?"

"I don't know... something about using the energy from pain to your advantage."

"Exactly, work with that. Try."

"Okay." Kya closed her eyes and took five deep breaths. She focused on the pain at the back of her head and felt the hurtful energy pulsing out from it. She imagined it being caught by a butterfly net and whispered a healing spell into its swirls. The cut closed up even though her hair remained a bloody sticky mess. "It worked," Kya said, "I feel much better."

Cameron was relieved, "Good. Let's go." He led the way down the winding staircase and stopped when they reached the bottom. There was a group of guards in the large open area up ahead. "We need to create a distraction," Cameron told Kya.

"I've got an idea," Kya replied and pointed at a sleeping guard against one of the walls. Kya whispered a spell. The guard started floating up and as soon as he opened his eyes he started screaming for help. His clothes all came off and started dancing around him and tying him up into a cocoon. He pulled two of his arms free and tried ripping the clothes off the rest of his body but the clothes stuck fast like glue. For a Thyrexian with five arms, three legs, and a spiked tail, Kya thought he'd be a little tougher.

More guards came running in to help, and they tried to wrench the first one back to the ground but nothing worked. Cameron tried putting the same enchantment on the other guards so that Kya wouldn't get tired out. It worked, and at Cameron's cue, Kya ran out unseen and slipped into a small crevice in the rock wall. Now that she was hidden, Kya cast a spell on her eyes to let her see through the mountain. She saw many twisting and turning tunnels along with a pretty big room with a throne in it and a passage that lead down to a deep cavern. The nearest exit was down the hallway to their left and then at the end of another hallway to the right.

Kya left her vision enchanted and waved to Cameron who slipped past the levitated guards and followed her down the hallway to the left. They continued until they got to the second hallway and turned right. To their amazement, at the end of the hallway there was a glowing opening which lead right into a busy visitor's center with humans in it. They ran down the hallway and out the opening. It was the oddest thing emerging from a fortress of magical beings into a building for regular human tourists.

As they hurried across the visitor's center they bumped into an older lady who was obviously failing at trying to look younger. She wore pink high heels and a blue boa scarf with a purple long-sleeved dress. "Watch where you're going!" she said with a strong British accent.

They ran past her to the front entrance on the other side of the visitor center, but before they got outside two security guards grabbed them by the arms and pulled them into a small passageway. "Gå inte körs i korridorerna! Se skyltarna? Besvärande barn..." the fat one yelled at them in Swedish pointing to the "No Running" signs. The guards then shoved them off and out the front door.

They ran down all of the stairs built into the mountainside until they got to a parking lot with a sign that said "Välkommen till Dragon Mountain!" "Welcome to Dragon Mountain!" Four trolls in security uniforms emerged from the trees on both sides of the parking lot and started toward them, but from the way that people casually walked past them Kya could tell they had been enchanted to look like humans to non-magical beings.

"Come on!" Kya yelled and pulled Cameron between two SUVs. She saw a tour bus that had just arrived and had people pouring out of it. The trolls were advancing on them fast. Kya and Cameron kept running toward the bus when they noticed a familiar girl and older man being washed out in the flow of people.

"Eliza!" Kya screamed as Eliza looked around for where the voice was coming from. *How could she not notice us?* Kya thought as she screamed at Eliza again but it was too late, the trolls were upon them. Kya swung around and hit one in the face but it had no effect and he twisted her arm up her back. Kya screamed again and saw Eliza continue searching for the voices. No one else seemed to hear them.

Cameron enchanted one of the troll's pants so it lifted him into the air and gave him a wedgie. The troll screamed in a high-pitched voice as he grabbed at his pants trying to readjust them. Cameron then turned to one of the other trolls just in time to see the troll's fist slam into his face and knock him unconscious.

Kya was desperate for Eliza's help who had begun walking vaguely toward them. Kya used the pain

136

coming from her arm to cast a spell on Eliza's baseball hat that showed her all of Kya's memories regarding the mountain. Then they were carried away into a hidden entrance in the side of the mountain.

A cell in the mountain. Ogre guards. A throne room and a hidden cavern. A passage in the wall. Eliza knew where to go. "This way," she pulled Charles across the parking lot to the visitor's center. It was actually quite a nice place for what Kya's memories portrayed its secrets to be. With light green walls and several small exhibits on the mountain's history and features, the visitor's center was very normal, all except for the glowing hole in the wall on the far side of the main exhibit area.

"There. Follow me," Eliza pulled Charles toward the hole wondering why no one else was even curious as to where it led.

"Eliza, it's just a wall. There's nothing special about it," Charles stopped and refused to go forward any farther.

"It's a passage, can't you see it?"

"No it's not. There's just a wall there." Charles couldn't see what Eliza was seeing, but then again this had happened before where Charles couldn't see something because he was just a regular human.

"It must be hidden from you," Eliza decided. "Which probably means that you can't go through it. But I can." Eliza began walking into the wall.

"Eliza don't be silly. You're not going in there alone!" Charles tried to stop her but she just kept on walking, right into the side of Dragon Mountain. Eliza turned around and saw her grandfather looking for her as if she'd disappeared. She stuck her hand out and waved at him, hoping that he was the only one who saw it... but he wasn't.

An old Devalpa guard noticed the girl going into the passage that led into their fortress. He used his telepathy to contact the Progenitor about the girl. She would be found and either welcomed or destroyed.

Cameron woke up in a different cell than he had been in before. He had a splitting headache. He groaned and lifted a hand to touch his face. His left eye was swollen as big as a golf ball and his nose was still bleeding. Kya was sitting in the corner of the cell cross-legged with her eyes shifting from blue to aqua to bright green and back again.

"Kya," he shook her knee. Kya turned and looked at Cameron with her freaky eyes making him feel uncomfortable. It wasn't Kya looking at him that was for sure.

And then Kya spoke with a deep voice that was scarred with wisdom and loss, "My kind have waited a long time for you. They are in hiding but you are their key to escape. Your friend will be joining you very soon. You must help us. You have two days." Kya's eyes came back to normal and she asked Cameron if he'd heard that too.

"Yes, of course, you were the one talking."

"I was talking?"

"Yes that was you talking but—"

"No it was—"

"Get your filthy hands off me!!" they heard Eliza scream outside the cell door. "I will not be treated like this! You don't know who you're dealing with!"

Eliza squeezed her eyes shut but nothing happened. She opened her eyes and realized that she hadn't changed, "How come I didn't... I'm not..." she turned on the guard again with renewed anger. "What did you do to me?!?!?! You have no right to drag me in here! Are you deaf? Let me go!!!"

They shoved Eliza into the cell next to Kya and Cameron and locked the door. Eliza pressed herself up against the bars and screamed at the guards at the top of her lungs, "Don't think you're done with me!! Don't you dare walk away from me! You are the filthiest, ugliest, worst guards in this whole place! You'll never get a promotion and you're gonna be down here your whole life and you're gonna die as an old ugly troll cuz' I'm coming after you so you better watch out!" The guards closed the heavy metal door at the end of the hallway. Eliza was left panting against the bars of the cell door.

"You certainly have it out for them," Cameron said through the bars separating their cells.

"They better watch their backs," Eliza growled. Then she noticed Cameron's eye, "So what happened to you?"

"Failed escape attempt. Why are you here?"

"I followed a hole in the wall. Lone told me how to find this place, along with some of your other paintings Kya. And your spell on my hat was a great help. These caverns used to belong to the dragons and the Symbari took them away. The dragons can beat the Symbari but they need our help."

"Where exactly are we?" asked Kya.

"Switzerland, you didn't know?" Eliza responded a bit surprised.

"No, we were unconscious the whole way here."

"Huh, must have been pretty strong magic. Have you learned anything about these guys?" Eliza asked.

"They certainly have a lot of loyal followers and they're very powerful," Kya said. "At the museum when the Shadowed Man made me pass out, it was these people who sent him the power to do it. What we felt at the mall when they took us was the same magic, just on a much larger scale. I'm not sure what their objective is, but the only reason they aren't killing us is because they think they can somehow use us."

"For what?" Eliza asked. They were interrupted by the two guards that had just brought Eliza in. They burst through the outer doors and marched toward their cells. "Back for more?!" Eliza screamed at them. They unlocked Eliza's door and she was suddenly bound by ropes that seemed to come out of nowhere, without the guards even moving a muscle. The guards grabbed a loose end of the rope and pulled her out of her cell and then moved on to Kya and Cameron. They too were bound with the strange ropes and escorted out of their cell.

The ropes constricted their use of magic just like the bars had in their cells. The Symbari were more cautious now that they better understood the power of their captives.

They were brought up several flights of stairs and into a large room with doors on every side and a raised platform in the center with a man seated on a large throne made of black leather and silver. He had dreadlocks and a crazy look in his eyes that made him look like a psychopath. *This must be the Progenitor, the leader of the Symbari*, Kya thought to herself.

"What do you want us to do with them now Lord Zedoc?" one of the guards asked the man on the throne.

"I've decided they're more trouble than they're worth. Take them to the Taniwha," the dreadlocked man said with a wicked smile on his face and a wave of his hand.

Eliza remembered learning about the Taniwha from Hemlick. It was supposed to be just a legend. He said it was a reptile like creature that could change shape and lived in caves or near water. They were cousins of dragons and were described in myths as terrifying creatures that captured people... and then ate them.

Zedoc spoke to the guards again, "And take those hideous ropes off, I like to watch a fight."

CHAPTER 13
τ η ε τ α ν ι ω η α

"What's a Taniwha?" Cameron asked fearfully as they were shoved into a dimly lit room. The guards took the ropes off but the room was still restricting their magic.

"It's a dragon-like beast that can change shape. It eats people," Eliza said frankly. She tried to seem tough but she couldn't stop the worry from seeping into her expression.

The guards forced them into a narrow muddy tunnel and closed a heavy door behind them. The door disappeared and then the wall started moving toward them. There was no place to go except forward. They began to walk down the tunnel into the darkness with the walls just inches away on each side of them. The ceiling of the tunnel started getting lower, forcing them to stoop.

Eliza screamed as she slipped on the mud and began to slide down the slope of the tunnel. She knocked Kya and Cameron down who were walking in front of her and they were now all sliding down the ever steepening mud slide. The tunnel widened again and then emptied out into a muddy chamber where they all landed with a thud.

In the dim light of the chamber they could see the ground all around them littered with bones. They looked up and saw that they were in the corner of a huge underground cavern. A giant cliff jutted out from the wall to their left with a waterfall coming down it, fed by water flowing through a hole near the top of the cavern. Sunlight also shined through the hole at the top of the cavern and lit up the underground river flowing through the middle of the cavern. The light reflected off the stalactites and created a really beautiful scene if not for the creature leisurely walking toward them from the shadows.

Everyone was covered in mud and dazed from their ride down the slide but they immediately perked up when they saw the Taniwha. She really was beautiful as her scales shimmered with the light. If not for the ferocity in her eyes, she would have been a welcome sight. She was more of a serpent than a dragon. Dragons only have four legs and two wings, each about twice the size of their body. The Taniwha had eight legs, four on each side, and her wings were smaller, but there were four of them.

The Taniwha came closer and turned into a lion. "I'm trying to decide how to kill you," the Taniwha said, turning into a huge viper. "Quick or slow? How am I supposed to decide," the Taniwha changed into a bear. This time Eliza matched the Taniwha and became an exact replica of the grizzly bear the Taniwha had become.

The Taniwha hesitated then roared and changed into a rhino. Eliza did the same and the Taniwha let out a bloodcurdling squeal and changed back into her serpent form. Eliza followed her change but became a blue version. The Taniwha paced back and forth in front of Eliza looking her up and down. "How could they dare to put me up against one of my own?" she screamed. "They already know I hate doing this and this makes it so much harder!"

"Wait, you don't do this of your own free will?" Eliza asked, puzzled. *Why would a creature kill and eat other creatures if it didn't want to?* Eliza thought.

"No! Magical beasts taste terrible and it's like cannibalism. Cows and pigs are better. Sheep are a little chewy but it's better than eating your own kind."

"Then why do you do it?" Eliza changed back into herself.

Now the Taniwha looked terrified, "Because of the rain of fire. It rains a burning sheet over everything and my river evaporates until it is dry. That river is the only comfort I have and they take it away until I start dying and then they bring it back, but not until I am on the verge of death. Do you know what that's like? Being on the brink of death, hoping for death if it would only end the pain, and then they bring you back again? They flood my cavern with water until I am rejuvenated and then threaten me with the rain of fire again." A low rumbling sound came from above and small stones rained down on their shoulders. "The fire is coming!" the Taniwha screamed and lunged at them with all her might, sadness in her eyes that she had to kill them for her own life.

They dodged the Taniwha's attack and started to run toward the cliff face leading up to the opening near the top of the cavern. More rock fell from the ceiling, smashing on the ground between them and the Taniwha, giving them a sizable head start. The Taniwha went around the rocks, transforming into a cheetah and gaining on them fast. They scrambled up a rocky hill to the bottom of the cliff face with the waterfall cascading down to their right.

When the Taniwha saw what they were doing, she changed herself into an ape for better climbing. Zedoc also saw what they were doing and decided to accelerate the rain of fire. It began to fall at the far end of the subterranean chamber and work its way toward them.

Kya, Cameron, and Eliza climbed up the cliff face toward the opening above. The mist from the waterfall was soaking them through and the wet rock was slippery and hard to grip. The Taniwha reached the bottom of the cliff quicker than they thought and started using her long feet and arms to maneuver up the cliff face. Eliza could have changed into an ape too, but she would have just left her friends behind, so she kept climbing as fast as she could. They were almost to the top. The fire was halfway across the cavern.

When they reached the top of the cliff, they pulled themselves over the top and were ready to run free through the opening in the rock, but then it was like they hit a glass wall that closed in on all sides of them. They were frozen where they were by some kind of force field, unable to move in any direction.

Eliza had an idea and changed into a goat. She moved forward about a foot. She changed again into a mouse and moved forward again. Kya and Cameron were still stuck in the invisible force field.

Kya screamed at Eliza over the sound of the waterfall, "Every time you change, the field changes to keep you in. If you change fast enough, you might confuse it on what it's supposed to keep in and you might escape!" They were all soaking wet and their clothes were ripped jagged from the sharp edges of the cliff face.

"I can't leave you!" Eliza screamed back.

"Go! Find help! We'll catch up!" Kya gave Eliza a fake smile and a nod. Eliza took Kya's advice and changed into a lion and then a bear and then a cow and then a horse until she was changing shape so fast that Kya couldn't tell one animal from another. With every transformation, Eliza moved forward and soon enough she was free of the force field. Eliza turned and looked back at her friends. *They'll be fine...* she lied to herself. With a lump in her throat she waved goodbye and exited through the opening in the cavern. When she got outside, Eliza noticed another mountain to the south of the one she was on. *Maybe the Great Ones are there*, Eliza thought to herself. *They definitely aren't in this mountain.* Eliza took off running in the direction of the other mountain.

Kya felt an overwhelming sense of helplessness as she watched Eliza disappear through the opening and then turned around to see the Taniwha reach the ledge behind them.

"No escaping this time," the Taniwha panted. She turned into a huge black dog with red eyes and bared teeth.

"Wait!" Cameron said desperately. "You hate the fire. Right? Then go! Eliza made it out. So can you."

"I've tried a thousand times; no one can get past that force field," the Taniwha said, convinced she was stating a fact.

"Just change fast enough between every animal that you know. That's what Eliza did," Cameron replied.

This time the Taniwha perked up. "I never thought of trying that to escape, even though I've done it many times to my victims." Then she became suspicious. "How do I know you aren't trying to trick me?"

"Eliza's gone isn't she?" Cameron pointed out.

The Taniwha looked around and noticed the obvious. She walked up to the shield and immediately got stuck in it. She focused and transformed into a lion, then a bear, and then a parrot. Her transformations went faster and faster until she broke free of the shield. She howled in relief and ran in circles, so happy to be free again. She turned back to Kya and Cameron, "How can I repay you?"

"Find Eliza, help her figure out a way to take down the Symbari," Kya said. The Taniwha howled again, went through the opening, and bounded down the mountain after Eliza.

When the Taniwha was gone Kya and Cameron both tried to pull themselves away from the field but it proved to be impossible. The wall of fire was almost upon them.

Eliza had hiked for at least ten miles and was now ascending up a mountain to the South of Dragon Mountain. She had taken frequent breaks but every time she stopped for too long she heard something crashing through the brush behind her, so she had to keep moving. Her feet were dragging and she was using a tree branch as a walking stick for support.

She tripped on a rock and fell on her face. She slowly got back up and dragged herself over to lean against a tree. She had only meant to rest for a minute but she must have dozed off because she woke up with a big black dog licking her face.

"What are you doing up here?" Eliza asked, "Where's your owner?" She patted the dog on its head and slowly stood up, stretching her cramped muscles.

Then, to her surprise, the dog turned into a horse and neighed impatiently at Eliza. Her tired brain slowly comprehended why the animal's eyes looked so familiar. It was the Taniwha.

Eliza gasped and took a step backward, "Don't think you can trick me. What are you doing here?"

The Taniwha turned into a young woman with light brown hair and black eyes, "Your friends showed me how to get free like you did and they sent me to help you."

"How do I know you're not lying?"

The Taniwha hesitated, "I can show you my memories. As a magical being you know there's no way I can fake those."

"Okay," Eliza said.

The Taniwha put her hand on Eliza's shoulder and replayed the scene from when she got to the top of the cliff intending to kill Kya and Cameron, to her escape through the force field while Kya and Cameron were still trapped with the rain of fire approaching. When she finished there were tears in Eliza's eyes. Eliza nodded and wiped her nose on her sleeve.

"My name's Narissa by the way," the Taniwha said in a gentle voice.

"Eliza."

Chapter Thirteen

Narissa changed back into a white horse and Eliza climbed on. They worked their way up the mountain and after a while Eliza fell asleep against Narissa's neck. Narissa walked until dusk and then she woke Eliza up.

"We need to stop," Narissa said. "I won't be able to see anything pretty soon. We should find a place to sleep."

Eliza nodded groggily and climbed off Narissa's back. They walked a little farther and then night fell in the forest. It was almost pitch black with the light of a quarter moon casting dim shadows on the ground. As her eyes adjusted to the darkness Eliza noticed a glowing light not too far away, like a small town in the mountains. Why would there be a town so far away from the rest of civilization? Her curiosity won over her fatigue and they slowly headed toward the light.

The shadows stretched toward them as they made their way through the trees. The light grew brighter and brighter as they neared it but the brush around them grew darker and darker. Tree branches and thorns ripped at Eliza's clothing until one branch stuck to her shirt. The tension in the tree branch pulled her back towards the tree. Other branches clawed at her, ripping into her skin leaving bloody marks all over her body.

Narissa whinnied as the trees attacked her too. She bucked at the tree closest to her and bolted through the forest into the clearing that the light was coming from.

Eliza was being pulled deeper into the tree's embrace until she felt she was wrapped in a cocoon of branches so tight that she could barely breathe. A pair of red eyes appeared in front of her with a matching malicious smile.

"What have we here?" the tree boomed, rattling the ground around Eliza. Three other trees appeared around her, their eyes casting a red glow on Eliza like an evil, dramatic spotlight. "A little shapeshifter again? Ah, they are always my favorite prey," the first tree spoke again. The other hawthorn trees laughed at their leader's sinister taunt. "The last one we poked from a distance but this one I think we should do face to face. It's much more fun to see the fear in their eyes when they realize what's coming." The trees burst into uncontrollable laughter which shook Eliza up and down until she felt sick, like she might throw up.

But then their laughter quickly turned to horror as a crashing sound came through the trees behind them and a stronger, thicker tree pushed his way between two of the hawthorn trees.

"I told you to leave," the ash tree shouted at them. "And what do you do? You come back to annoy me some more. Let her go and never come back."

The hawthorn trees smiled feebly and were already backing away from the ash tree, "Hey, we meant no harm. We were just having a little fun. Right?" the leader said as he slowly set Eliza down on the ground and backed up farther.

"No way, you're a liar!" Eliza yelled as she changed into a porcupine. She shot quills at the hawthorn trees and they howled in pain, dragging their roots through the ground while they retreated into the distance, leaving a deep trench behind them. Eliza changed back into herself and lay limp on the ground.

The ash tree picked Eliza up in a small bed of leaves and carried her into the clearing where Narissa waited. In the center of the clearing was a huge oak tree that was at least seventy feet tall with several small rooms created by its branches. There were all kinds of little creatures living in its branches and groups of small trees were at its trunk listening to stories that he told with a booming voice.

All around the clearing were more trees: oak, ash, and holly, all of them had one or two little platforms in their branches.

The ash tree laid Eliza down on one of the platforms of a holly tree and left her to sleep. The wood from the tree branches grew up around Eliza creating a little room. Narissa changed herself into a bird and flew through the last opening in the branches before it closed up around Eliza, shutting off all sound from the clearing below.

CHAPTER 14

♍ ✔ ■ ♓ ○ ⫻ ■

Spits of fire were starting to hit the ground around
Kya and Cameron still frozen in the force field. The
torrential wall of fire was only seconds away. "If we can
bind our energies together then we might be able to
counter the force field enough to break free and find
cover under some rocks," Kya yelled to Cameron. They
reached for each other's hands and grabbed onto each
other. "On three, *secarithy myari vansthi.* One, two,
three!" They screamed the spell in unison and a huge
energy pulse burst outward, blowing rock debris
everywhere. It worked. They were free of the force field
and were about to dive for cover when Cameron
noticed a hidden tunnel that had opened up in the rock
just a few yards away.

Kya collapsed on the ground in exhaustion but
Cameron dragged her to her feet. "Come on! There's a

tunnel! Let's go." They helped each other to the mouth of the tunnel and quickly sealed it off behind them as they watched the last of the Taniwha's cavern being consumed by fire.

Kya began to pass out but Cameron caught her and laid her gently on the floor. Kya was unconscious but she would be okay. "We're safe for now," Cameron whispered to Kya even though he knew she could not hear him. "Eliza's getting help and hopefully the Symbari won't find us in here. Everything's going to be okay." He held onto Kya's hand and sat there looking up and down the tunnel for any signs of trouble.

Just as Cameron was drifting off to sleep, the sound of feet running down the tunnel woke him up. He immediately hopped to his feet and readied himself. As soon as he saw someone come around the corner he shot an enchanted rock at them and slammed them into the wall. He was surprised to see that it was a girl. Another girl came from around the corner and made a shield for the first one who was just getting up and brushing herself off. Cameron ran forward, breaking the shield around the first girl and punching the second girl in the nose. *I'm really getting the hang of this magic stuff!* he thought, until a third girl from the shadows shot a dart into Cameron's shoulder, paralyzing him. He was frozen from the neck down. "Don't touch her!" Cameron screamed at the first two girls as they walked wearily past him and began to pick up Kya. The third girl approached Cameron cautiously as if she wasn't sure that the dart had worked.

"Can you move at all?" she asked, curling her black hair behind her ear. Her eyes were brown and she wore combat boots, a dark blue shirt, and cargo pants. She also had an ammo belt filled with darts of what seemed like a million different colors and shapes.

"No, what do you think?" Cameron replied.

"I wasn't sure. We don't want to hurt you. The dart caused you no pain, am I correct?"

"That's correct," Cameron said slowly, "I just can't move."

"We will take you to our camp. We won't hurt your girlfriend."

"She's not my girlfriend," Cameron felt his cheeks grow hot.

"Okay then, your friend, but when we take the dart out you have to promise that you won't try to hurt us.

You can easily overpower us so I need to know that you trust us."

Cameron was cautious, "Okay but what do you want us for anyway?"

"We don't *want* you for anything. We're trying to help you. We call ourselves Canimon. Most of us are escaped prisoners but some are Symbari guards who have defected and give us an inside eye on things. We don't like the Symbari either."

Cameron nodded and the girl pulled the dart out of his arm, "I'm Olivia, captain of the Canimon Blue Squad, nice to meet you."

"I'm Cameron, and sorry about the rock and all, I thought you girls were the Symbari." They shook hands.

"No problem, my girls are tough. This is Emma and Abigail. They're two of my toughest." The two girls nodded at Cameron. They both wore the same outfit as Olivia except their shirts were a lighter blue and their ammo belts had some sort of energy pellets in them. Cameron noticed that Olivia had a few of those too. They carried Kya past Olivia and Cameron and around the corner. One held Kya's torso and carefully cradled her head while the other held her legs.

"Will she be okay?" Cameron asked about Kya.

"She's very strong. She must have thought the force field was stronger than it was and used a little of her life energy to defeat it. It will come back with rest. I'm guessing she isn't used to using her life energy. She probably uses the energy from her gherons and the magic in her spells to get things done. That's why using so little of her life energy took that much out of her."

Cameron nodded in agreement. They followed the first two girls down many passages. At one of the forks in the passages, they turned left while Cameron noticed a carving in the wall on the right tunnel that pointed forward and a carving on the left tunnel that pointed to the right tunnel.

"Shouldn't we have gone down that other tunnel?" Cameron asked, "That's where both arrows pointed."

"No," Emma said. Emma had blonde hair and striking blue eyes. Her skin was much paler than the other girls, who looked to be some mix of Asian and Indian. "We try to confuse people coming in here so that it's really hard to find our camp. These were the dragon council's secret corridors and they had traps everywhere. Nothing would kill you, but you would be captured so they could evaluate your intentions. Everyone in our rebellion that has to navigate the tunnels has to pass a rigorous test to make sure they won't get lost and set off a trap."

"Impressive," Cameron said in admiration.

"Thank you," Emma replied. They walked for another ten minutes and then ran into a larger tunnel bustling with people. As they walked down into the flow of people, a path slowly opened up through the crowd as if having unconscious people come in was an everyday routine to them. They moved through the crowd quickly and into a cavern even larger than the Taniwha's. There were tents set up everywhere and most people that they saw were making more tents. Cameron saw weapons in almost everyone's belts and knew they had the beginnings of an army.

Kya's head was sore and all of her limbs felt like jello. She moaned and started to roll over, almost into the campfire.

"Whoa girl, just relax, let's get you some soup," a girl with blond hair and bright blue eyes came over and helped prop her up against a large rock. "I'm Emma." Kya nodded at her but her throat was so parched she couldn't say a word. Emma brought her a bottle full of water and a bowl of chicken noodle soup with chunks of something that Kya didn't recognize.

"Thank you," Kya said after taking several gulps of water and eating half the soup. Her hands were still shaking from her weakness. "Where am I?"

"You're in the Canimon camp. We are all rebels against the Symbari," Emma laughed nervously. "Though none of us could have done what you did."

Kya was confused, "What did I do?"

"Here, we filmed it on one of our cameras that we have in the Taniwha's cave. It's a little fuzzy though from the energy waves that you sent out." Emma grabbed a laptop out of her shoulder bag and brought up a video that looked like it was shot from right above the tube that the Taniwha's victims fall out of.

The camera zoomed in on Kya and Cameron at the top of the ledge. All of a sudden huge waves of green energy shot out and destroyed everything around them.

Half the cliff began to fall in a landslide and the remaining rock walls in the Taniwha's cavern collapsed inward. Cameron helped Kya over to the tunnel that had opened up in the wall and they disappeared into the mountain. Then the view switched to a camera inside the tunnel Kya and Cameron had escaped into, showing Cameron gently laying Kya down on the ground and holding her hand, followed by the fight that ended with Cameron realizing what was going on, and then the journey to the main camp.

"He really cares about you, you know," Emma said, taking her computer back and stowing it.

This took Kya by surprise, "We've never been anything more than friends." But this started Kya thinking. Could Cameron really think of her as more than just a friend? No, she would have done the same for him... as a friend.

Emma nodded at a campfire a little ways away. Kya looked over and saw Cameron sitting with a bunch of other guys around a small table. He was focusing on a piece of paper but he glanced up at Kya to make sure she was okay and when he saw that she was awake he clearly showed his relief. The other guys followed his gaze and Kya waved at them. They all burst out laughing and Cameron turned bright red. Kya giggled.

"You see what I mean?" Emma said. "He's been constantly asking about you in all his free time."

"Look, there's nothing between us. We're just really good friends."

"Whatever you say."

"I'm serious!"

"Okay. I get it, you're just friends." Emma wasn't very convinced.

"I'm going to walk around," Kya said as she got up and propped herself against a rock until her head stopped spinning.

"Are you sure you'll be okay? I could go with you," Emma offered.

Kya thought about it, "Okay, I guess a little company wouldn't hurt."

Emma hopped up and checked the energy pellets in her guns, "Okay, I'm ready to go." They walked side by side down the subterranean road they were camped next to and turned onto a quieter side road.

Then Kya remembered something about the video. "How did we destroy so much rock? I mean, I didn't think we were that strong."

Emma looked at her with surprise, "You barely used any of your life energy Kya. Compared to your energy, everyone else here is nothing. If you learned to use the energy you have, you could cause a phenomenal amount of damage."

Kya let that sink in. She might be able to defeat the Symbari with that kind of power. "But, wouldn't it kill me? Using all that life energy?"

Emma shook her head, "Not if you practiced. We can do some warm ups right now if you want. During our training we practice using only our life energy. The more we get used to using our life energy the less it hinders us when we use it. That way we aren't immobilized every time we use a large amount of life energy in battle."

"I think I should wait until I'm a little stronger," Kya replied.

"Good idea. Let's go to the traders market. Even though we're basically an army, the girls among us still love to shop!" Emma took Kya to a cluster of little stalls selling scarves. Emma began to barter with them for the price of a beautiful blue scarf that matched the color of her shirt. After she got it in return for three feet of orange cloth that she had in her backpack, she turned to Kya and asked if she wanted anything.

"Oh no, I'm okay. I don't have anything to trade anyway."

"I'll start you off," Emma insisted. She pulled a dirty belt from her bag and gave it to an old man who in turn gave her a muddy headband. "Just trade this for some other stuff and you'll be good to go," she gave Kya the headband. "I'll meet up with you at the fortuneteller's tent in half an hour. Good luck!" Emma said as she pointed toward the fortuneteller's tent. With that Emma disappeared into the throng of people.

"Well, I guess I better get started," Kya murmured to herself. She went to the nearest shop and showed them her headband. The woman nodded and showed her a thin silver chain. They traded and Kya moved on to the next stall. The man looked at Kya's silver chain and offered her a little flower charm. Kya agreed and they exchanged their items.

"Not gonna happen Fredrick," an unfamiliar, but friendly voice said from behind Kya. She turned and saw a tall guy with black hair, green eyes, and a nice smile. "You owe her at least two more charms," the good looking guy said to the trader. "That chain she gave you doesn't have a scratch on it." Fredrick looked very unhappy about being exposed but gave Kya two more charms. "And don't try that again, I'm watching you."

What a nice person, Kya thought, observing the stranger who had kept the man honest. Kya followed him away from the stall and tapped him on the shoulder, "Thank you for that."

"No problem, Fredrick has been robbing people of their trades for a while and I've been keeping an eye on him." He stuck out his hand, "I'm Ethan."

"Kya," she shook Ethan's hand. He seemed taken aback by her name.

"Not the 'Kya' I've been hearing about are you?"

"I don't know, what have you been hearing?" They began to walk down the street.

"I heard that she blew up the force field that no one has found a way to counter. She was so powerful that she almost completely destroyed the Taniwha's cavern."

Kya laughed, "Sounds about right."

"So you are the famed Kya?"

"Yes, I guess so."

"Let me buy you something."

"No I don't need anything."

"Come on, it would be an honor," Ethan bowed at the waist.

Kya gave in, "Fine."

"So what do you want?" Ethan asked.

"Umm, something useful?"

"So... armor, weapon, a holster?"

"You tell me, you seem to be part of the army here, aren't you?"

Ethan laughed, "I am captain of the Red Squad, the team everyone calls when they need the best of the best."

"What's with all of these squads and colors?" Kya asked.

"Colors show rank, it goes red, orange, blue, green, black, yellow, purple, pink. Each color also means

170

something about the level of danger something is. For example, if there's been an intelligence leak about where Canimon forces are positioned, then we would send in Purple with their mind wiping unit. But if Zedoc acted on that information and his army broke into one of our caverns, we would deploy the whole Red and Orange Squads."

Kya nodded to show that she understood. They kept on walking until Ethan led her to a small stand where they sold jackets. He bought her a dark green one with two brown patches on the elbows.

"It gets really cold down here at night," Ethan said. Kya put it on and immediately warmed up. She told Ethan about her appointment at the fortuneteller's tent and they started to head in that direction.

On the way there, Kya spotted Cameron and he started toward them. But when Cameron noticed Ethan he unconvincingly pretended to see someone else and branched off onto another path.

"Who's that?" Ethan asked.

"Cameron. He came with me. We've been friends for a long time, we're really close," Kya said.

"Well I hope you're not too close for my sake."

"Just friends," Kya laughed at Ethan's flirty comment.

They arrived at the fortuneteller's tent. It had a second tent attached to the back for storage. They stopped in front where Emma was waiting. Emma seemed surprised to see Ethan but not pleasantly. She said hello as politely as she could and then pulled Kya aside for a private conversation.

"What is *he* doing here?" she hissed, gripping Kya's arm.

"I met him on the way," Kya said.

"Please, don't ever hang out with him again."

"Why?" Kya asked.

"He can't be trusted," Emma was obviously very mad, for what reason Kya could not imagine. Emma saw her confused expression and explained a little bit more. "We've had a few super powerful people like you come along but they were all murdered and a lot of us think Ethan had something to do with it. Either he found their body or he was with them when a supposed Symbari assassin showed up. It can't be a coincidence that he's there every time. The only reason he has stayed a commander is because there's been no solid evidence against him, just him being in the immediate vicinity when all of these people who could have helped us died."

"He seems really nice; he even made sure I wasn't cheated when I was trading," Kya pointed out.

"He always does that kind of stuff, but please, try to stay away from him. I don't want you to get hurt." Emma's voice and expression was so earnest and concerned. Kya nodded and pushed aside her thoughts about Ethan for later.

A tall man ran out of the fortuneteller's tent screaming with tears running down his face. He fell to his knees in the middle of the street, "Please no! I'm not ready to die! I have a family, I still need time!" A motorcar came racing down the street toward him. He was rooted to the spot screaming but the motorcar swerved around him as the driver hung out the window cursing at him for being an idiot.

"I never said you were gonna die you dimwit! I meant you shouldn't be so cocky!" a chubby woman wearing a long flowing dress with a head wrap and a number of necklaces said as she emerged from the tent and yelled at the confounded man. The woman pulled her shawl tight around her, "What do you think I meant when I said you shouldn't value your life so much. You didn't even let me finish!" Then she noticed Emma, Kya, and Ethan. "Oh! Come to have your fortune told have you? Come inside, it's cold out here." She ducked into her tent and Emma followed her but Ethan grabbed Kya's arm right as she was about to enter.

"I've got to go, there's a training class that starts in ten minutes," Ethan said.

"Okay, see you later," Kya tried to go into the tent but Ethan wouldn't let go of her arm.

"Whatever Emma told you about me is a lie," Ethan said, "She's hated me ever since I got promoted from the Blue Squad and she didn't."

"Okay, I got it, see you later," Kya wrenched her arm free and went into the fortuneteller's tent but not before seeing an angry look cross Ethan's face.

The fortuneteller sat opposite the table from Kya and gathered her robes around her. Emma sat to the left of Kya, her eyes flickering between Kya and the fortuneteller, watching for any movement from the two.

The fortuneteller stared at Kya with an unwavering gaze that made most people nervous, but Kya stared right back. The fortuneteller finally broke the silence, "You have a soul of magic."

Kya nodded but said nothing. The only noise was the sound of Emma's nervous shifting.

The fortuneteller pulled out an old jade bracelet that had a dull shine to it and dark blue engravings that read ⌐ ■ ⌐ ✕ ℔ ◣ , which meant 'energy' in Reesk. "This is extra energy. My family has been putting energy into it for generations and there's no telling how much is in there now. Use it before you use your life energy. The coming battle is close at hand." The fortuneteller placed the bracelet in Kya's hand and curled Kya's fingers around it. She patted Kya's fist and shooed them away, retreating to her tent in the back.

Kya opened her fist to look closer at the bracelet the fortuneteller had given her. It had many colors of green and they swirled and shifted across the stone. As Kya slipped it over her wrist, the bracelet sent a surge of energy up her arm. Kya wrote a small note expressing her thanks to the fortuneteller and left it on the table, then they left the tent.

Kya and Emma found Cameron waiting impatiently outside. "I was wondering when you'd come out," Cameron said. "You've been in there for half an hour."

Has it really been that long? Kya thought. *It seemed like it only took a few minutes.* "Wow," Kya said aloud, "I guess that fortuneteller woman is used to people caving in quickly in her staring contests."

"What do you mean?" Cameron asked.

"I'm gonna go get myself some hot chocolate," Emma excused herself.

"Okay, see you later," Kya said. She turned back to Cameron and they started walking down a path. "The fortuneteller was staring at me intensely. I kept expecting her to do something but she didn't. She just sat there and stared at me. It was kind of disturbing, like she was looking into my soul and going through all my magical abilities."

"And what did you do?" Cameron asked.

"I stared right back. I guess I didn't want her to think that I was like everyone else and just looking at her kept me feeling confident. I think most people would have broken down and asked her to stop."

"And then you just left? You just stared at each other and left?"

"No, she gave me this," Kya held up her wrist to show Cameron the bracelet. "It has generations of her family's energy stored in it. I don't even get why she gave it to me. What am I to her?"

"Apparently you're pretty important. Everyone here seems to think so."

"Yeah, I know. Did you see the footage of what we did when we escaped from the rain of fire? I can't believe we did that. I mean, we're not that special compared to other magical beings."

"I wouldn't think so either but this whole place seems to believe that we can lead them to victory. I don't know if I'm up for that."

"I don't think I am either," Kya said.

"Well, we'll just have to play the part won't we?" Cameron replied.

"Sure, I guess."

Just then a group of boys who were gathered by some crates on the side of the road whistled at Kya.

They all laughed and their leader winked at Kya. But their smiles vanished as the dirt rose from the ground around them and swirled into a mini tornado, leaving them coughing and covered in dust from head to toe.

Kya was surprised and looked at Cameron who had a big grin on his face. Then the leader of the group screamed, "Get them!"

"Run!" Cameron yelled and led the way as they bolted down a side alley, laughing all the way.

CHAPTER 15

✔ ◀ ✔ ⊃⌐ ■ ⅟ ■ ℣ ▲ ♒︎⌐ ♎ ✕ ✔ ℣ ⫻ ■ ◆

The huge oak tree seemed very distraught over Eliza's simple request. He was usually very cheery and his darkened mood disturbed the other trees, who now gave him more than enough space to think.

Eliza tried to explain why the trees should take her to the dragons known as the Great Ones. "We need their help more than ever. Surely they would be angry if no one informed them that they were needed. They are referred to as the Great Ones so wouldn't they be more than happy to help?" But the oak tree didn't seem to want to disturb the Great Ones in their time of recuperation from the disease that had injured and weakened them.

"They are still strong but they are much weaker than they used to be. I fear that they will be destroyed in any battle because they have not risen to their full strength," the oak tree said.

"They don't have to fight; they could just lend us some power. They're in danger too. If they don't fight, they will be destroyed anyway. The Symbari don't plan to take prisoners."

The oak tree ruminated on this idea for quite a long time and no one dared to disrupt his silence. Finally he said, "You may talk to them."

Eliza nodded. She watched as the oak tree chanted an ancient rhythm and some of the older ash trees pounded on their trunks, adding to the beat:

They come
Bum, bum, bum
They come
Bum, bum, bum
They cast away the darkness
and replenish all the light
They come
Bum, bum, bum
They come

The oak tree chanted the song over and over with more and more trees joining in the call. The ground shook with the beat of the song and the voices of the trees. The air in front of the oak tree shimmered with energy and a pitch black window opened up in front of Eliza. The song stopped and everyone watched. Nothing moved.

"Did it work?" Eliza asked. Before she could ask again a pair of green eyes, shimmering with knowledge and power, appeared in the window making Eliza jump back.

A dim glow filled the window and a black dragon emerged from the shadows, staring out at Eliza with a questioning glare. "Who is this, Fragimond?" he asked the oak tree by his first name.

"She wishes to speak with you. She came from Dragon Mountain where you originally dwelled. She says that a group has taken over all of the remnant power you left there and is planning some kind of attack," Fragimond explained nervously.

"Yes," Eliza stepped forward, shaking with fear. The black dragon was very majestic to look at, but she knew he could probably kill her in the blink of an eye. "I was one of their prisoners myself but I escaped because I'm a shapeshifter and I tricked one of their force fields."

"And why should we help you?" the black dragon inquired. "This has nothing to do with us; we aren't even at half our power. We can't just destroy anything as we used to."

Eliza raised her voice and yelled at the dragon, "The Symbari will either destroy you in your sleep tonight or destroy you fighting for your life. But there is a slim chance we might win if we work together. Without you we're basically marching to our deaths. My friends are dead and the Symbari are not going to get away with it if I can help it." Everyone stared open mouthed at Eliza's boldness. No one ever yelled at the dragons like that.

But the black dragon seemed to perk up when Eliza mentioned the word Symbari and her outburst seemed to gain Eliza his approval. "I need to know what happened to your friends."

Eliza told the dragon about having to leave Kya and Cameron behind in the rain of fire in the Taniwha's cavern. The dragon listened intensely and then his eyes turned blue with swirling aqua patterns in them. A second window appeared next to the dragon's window. It showed a view from the top of a large cavern in the middle of Dragon Mountain. The window zoomed in on two people running from a group of boys.

Eliza almost screamed in excitement. Kya and Cameron were alive! They weren't hurt or in danger and they were even happy! Her eyes started to water and Eliza turned to the dragon, "Can I talk to them?"

"No, I won't be able to make contact because they don't know how to hold the connection. They aren't advanced enough to understand what the sound in their heads means. I'm sorry."

"It's okay," Eliza said.

The dragon's eyes turned back to their normal color and the window showing Kya and Cameron vanished. "We will help you," the dragon said. "I sensed a lot of power in your friends even through that feeble link and I could tell that camp they were in was preparing an army to battle the Symbari. The Symbari will be attacked from the inside and the outside tonight. You must come with me."

Eliza was confused but the window got bigger and bigger until it engulfed her, and soon she was inside a giant cavern standing in front of the black dragon. The clearing of trees she had been standing in could be seen in the portal hovering a few feet off the ground behind her. She turned and saw Narissa nod at her before the portal closed.

The black dragon lit the torches in the cavern around him with a flick of his claw. Thousands of dragons could be seen in their cubbies in the wall, awakening at his thunderous roar. There were so many colors and shades moving down walkways and out of the cubbies that it looked like a giant, liquidy rainbow.

The black dragon roared again and all the dragons stopped to watch him. "We are the Great Ones," he said solemnly.

"And we rule with wisdom," the other dragons answered back.

"Now it is time for us to rule with power," the black dragon said. "This young girl has escaped from a group called Symbari." The dragons whispered at the mention of Symbari. The black dragon continued, "And you can tell by their name that they use the magic we outlawed so long ago, the magic that used to control life. It is dangerous but this group has unearthed it and plans to rule above us. It is time for us to use our power to protect all life from them. Since we are not at our full

184

strength, I have chosen to use the Jade Dragon to aid us in our fight. Who is with me?"

The dragons all roared in response.

"Keep in mind that we must refill the Jade Dragon with energy after we win and during that time we will have much less power to defend ourselves against any remaining foes. But are we willing to take that risk?" The dragons roared again.

"Will we win?"

The dragons roared the loudest this time and Eliza quickly plugged her ears even though it barely made a difference.

"There is an army ready to attack our foes from inside Dragon Mountain and we must join them," the black dragon said. "Get ready for battle, we leave soon." The dragons burst into more noise as they hurried into their chambers to get their armor and extra energy.

Eliza followed the black dragon down a passage. She felt downsized by the huge dragons all around her so she turned into a dragon herself. She was dark blue with a hint of sea green. At first the dragons were surprised when she turned into one of them but then they went back to their business.

"So, what do I call you?" Eliza asked the black dragon, "I'm not going to call you dragon because that's like calling me human all the time."

"Velkador," the black dragon said.

"Ooh, cool. I'm Eliza, kind of boring compared to your name."

"Names mean little to us, we know each other by our colors and actions. That is what we base our names off of. I was not born Velkador, Velkador is what I became. It means 'powerful mystery' in Symbari. It represents my soul and character, and it can change with me. If I all of a sudden become happy and dumb then my name would be Domcrini."

Velkador turned into a smaller cavern with a huge dragon in the center. When they got closer, Eliza realized it wasn't really a dragon, it was a statue of a dragon made of jade. In fact, Eliza now realized that almost everything around her was made of jade.

"Why is everything jade around here?" Eliza asked, referring to the jade platforms, statues, and stones.

"Jade is a stone that can hold energy very well. It doesn't let the energy leak out like sparkling crystals do. It holds energy better than any other stone in the universe." Velkador walked up to the shimmering statue and placed his nose at the foot of it. Velkador's nose gleamed where it touched the statue and the jade dragon's mouth opened, releasing a flood of energy into the air. The energy spread into the walls of the chamber around them and went outward from there, sending energy to every dragon in the mountain.

Velkador pulled his nose away. With a smirk on his lips and fire in his eyes he grunted, "*Now* we're ready for battle."

CHAPTER 16

⌂ ﹌ Γ ◂ ✔ ✕ ♌ Γ ♑ ♓ ■ ◆

Cameron pulled Kya around the corner and into the shadows of the wall. He cracked open a passage in the wall and jumped inside, closing it up after Kya leapt in next to him. They heard the gang of boys run into the dead end and stumble to a stop. Cameron heard Kya stifle her laughter.

"Where'd they go?" the leader said. They walked around for a while kicking the ground and then wandered off back to town.

Cameron unsealed the wall and they climbed out of the crevice, finally letting their giggles free.

"You didn't have to do that little dust tornado trick you know," Kya said sitting down against the wall. She paused, "Did you see their faces?" Cameron nodded with a smile and they both burst out laughing again. Cameron slid down to sit next to Kya.

Their laughter faded but they still lingered on the moment. Cameron broke the silence, "Who was that guy who was with you before you went to the fortuneteller?"

Kya's mood darkened, "Oh, his name is Ethan. He's the captain of the Red Squad, the highest ranking squad in the army. He seems pretty nice but some people think he's been involved in some murders. Emma warned me about him, I don't think he's trustworthy." Kya went on about her talk with Ethan at the front of the fortuneteller's tent and the dirty look on Ethan's face.

"So are you two friends or what?" Cameron asked.

Kya shook her head no, then a grin crossed her face, "You're not jealous are you?" she teased.

"No," Cameron turned red. "I was just wondering—"

"You *are* jealous. You want me all to yourself; I'm not allowed to have any other guy friends."

"No, I—"

"You hate the idea of me even talking to another guy don't you?" Kya smiled and raised an eyebrow.

"Not true!"

"Yes it is!"

"No, it's not!"

"Yes it is!" Kya laughed and tapped Cameron on the head.

Cameron was about to let out some smart retort but before he could say it Kya stiffened. "What?" Cameron asked. Kya gagged and her hands went to her throat. She pushed against the wall and gasped for breath but nothing entered her lungs.

Cameron kneeled next to Kya as she rolled over onto the ground. "What's wrong?"

Kya rocked back and forth, opening and closing her mouth trying to breathe. A million thoughts flashed through Kya's head. *I can't breathe. Why can't I breathe? I've never forgotten how to breathe. Someone must be doing this. It's magic. Who...? Ethan!*

She looked around as fast as she could even with her fading vision. And then she saw it, the fingers of a hand reaching around the corner of the wall. She slowly pointed at it and with the last of her energy shot a bullet of power at the wall right next to the hand. The rock shattered in Ethan's face and sent him reeling backward, losing his focus on Kya. Kya took a deep breath and rolled onto her other side in relief.

Cameron watched the bullet of power hit the rock and took Kya's lead. He jumped to his feet. If Ethan tried to kill one of his friends, he was going to pay. Cameron pulled huge chunks of rock out of the walls and built a rock cage around Ethan as he lay stunned on the ground.

And then there was silence. Ethan was trapped by the large rocks surrounding him. Kya was starting to get her breath back. Cameron was standing by Ethan's rock cage, exhausted.

Then Ethan blew the rocks apart and rose from the ground. "You can't beat me. I've killed far better than you. Compared to them, you're both as pitiful as a bug." Ethan turned his fist and Kya's head twisted at a bad angle. Pain arced up her spine before she pulled herself out of the spell and back to normal.

Cameron rushed Ethan to tackle him but Ethan countered with a kick to the stomach. Cameron fell backward onto the ground.

Kya pulled herself to her knees and pointed her index finger at Ethan, who was towering over Cameron.

Balling her other hand into a fist and turning it in circles, Kya focused on Ethan's energy and tied it into painful knots in his head. Ethan cried out in pain and turned to Kya, fury in his eyes. He threw a wave of air at Kya and she went flying and tumbling face first into the wall.

Kya snarled and wiped her bloody nose, climbing to her feet, swaying unsteadily, "You're the pitiful little bug here Ethan. You've been reporting to the Symbari for quite a long time now haven't you?"

"Oh, so now the bug thinks she's smart. Well think again, because if you think you can win, then you're fooling yourself."

Kya was boiling with anger now and just when she'd made up her mind to use her life energy to kill Ethan, even if it killed her too, the bracelet on her wrist sent a wave of energy up her arm. It was almost like the bracelet was saying, *I'm here. Don't forget me. Use me instead. I want to help.* Kya focused carefully on one of the beads on the bracelet and felt so much energy come flooding out of it that she almost lost her balance and fell over as it rushed toward Ethan in a huge ball of white flame and engulfed him in energy.

Ethan screamed in anguish and thrashed about as the fire sapped his energy, leaving him lying on the ground as the fire died out. He panted heavily and looked like he was about to fall asleep but he fought to stay awake.

Kya stalked over to Ethan and said, "Who's the bug now, Ethan?" She went through all the reasons in her mind on why she should kill him right then and there but she couldn't bring herself to do it. "I'm not going to kill you," Kya fumed. "But I'm not going to cut you any slack either. You used your words to charm me, and you used your magic to try to kill me. Which one do you want to go first?"

Ethan was defiant and manipulative. "You're not really going to do this Kya. You know you can't. You aren't strong enough. You wouldn't strip anyone of their best traits out of anger would you?"

Would I? thought Kya. *Maybe I can't do this. Maybe he's right. I would really be killing his soul because he would never be able to go back to what he was.* Kya realized he was charming her again and she shook the thoughts away. "Salimeira cansi donch touncan spak," she said. As Ethan realized what she was doing he felt a searing pain deep in his throat and then it was over.

"Wad did you do you siwy giwl. You can'd do anyting at awl." After Ethan realized what he sounded like he was ashamed he'd even said anything at all.

Kya smiled sweetly at Ethan, "I'm sorry, I'm not quite sure what you're trying to say. Now, one down, one to go."

"Don't! I won't do anyting at awl! I pwomise! Pwease! I—," but Kya was already starting the spell.

"Symada cayhont nouda-reesk nouda-symbari nouda-amatition faritiont."

Ethan felt his life energy soaring back up and thought that Kya had messed the spell up, but he reached for power from other things and found that he could not get any. His magic was gone; he would forever be normal and crippled in speech.

Cameron walked up next to Kya and looked down at Ethan, "What should we do with him?"

"Call the Orange Squad; they'll deal with him. Have the Blue Squad look through his team, others might be working for the Symbari too." Cameron nodded and left to go talk to the Canimon leaders while Kya kept watch over Ethan until the Orange Squad arrived.

"You reawy tink you've won don't you?" Ethan eventually said, grinning and sitting up. "You tink you won't have a pwobwem anymore. You are so ignowant. To tink we didn't have a backup. Dey are on dier way wite now." Just then the wall behind Kya exploded and threw her into the air. She hit the ground with a thump and shielded herself from the debris raining around her. She rolled to her feet and watched as a dark army emerged through the dust and began to charge toward the camp.

"No," Kya whispered to herself, "No!" She pushed off the ground leaping into the air and flew up over the camp, dropping down right in the center where the squad leaders were gathered. "They're here," Kya gasped. "They broke through the east wall. Thousands, we have to stop them!"

Cameron heard the explosion behind him and felt it shake the ground. He started running back to help Kya but saw the green streak of magic fly over the camp and knew it must be her, so he continued heading to the center of camp. A short time later, Canimon soldiers started running past Cameron in the opposite direction toward the explosion. He stopped one of them and asked if he knew what the explosion was.

"The Symbari, most likely," the soldier replied. "So much for us attacking first. Our plans must have been betrayed. We're on our way to check it out."

Cameron thanked the soldier and started running faster toward the center of camp. He noticed that everyone running in the opposite direction had full body armor and weapons, so he decided his first stop should be to get some for himself.

When Cameron reached the center of camp, the word had already spread that the Symbari attack was confirmed. After a few minutes of looking around, Cameron found the armory tent. He went in and found rows and rows of breastplates, shin guards, shoulder pads, steel gloves, and weapons running the length of the oversized tent.

"Are you lookin' for anything special?" the blacksmith in charge of the armory tent asked in a gruff voice.

"Um, not really, just some protection and something I can use to fight with I guess. Let's focus on protection first."

"Good idea," the blacksmith replied. "Well then, you'd probably be a three and a half chest plate, fifteen inch shin plates, eh, maybe twenty. And if you want a helmet you look like a four or five but I'll warn you they're quite uncomfortable and heavy."

"Alright then, um, let's forget the helmet," Cameron decided. They walked around the shop trying on different pieces of armor, some fitting comfortably and some being discarded. Finally Cameron was all fitted for battle. The only thing missing was a weapon.

"What do you like to fight with?" the blacksmith asked.

"I usually fight with magic so I'm not sure what kind of a weapon I'd like or anything, um, I probably won't use it correctly but I'll take anything you've got."

The blacksmith pulled out a long sword with a blue handle. "See how this one feels."

Cameron held the sword with both hands but it still felt heavy. The blue ribbon wrapped around the hilt was rough and hard to hold. "I think I'll try a different one," Cameron said.

The blacksmith took the sword back and pulled out a shorter sword with red designs on the blade. It had a ruby set into the hilt and the handle was covered in black velvet. Cameron thought the sword looked beautiful even though it was menacing. He could hold it easily in one hand and it was balanced perfectly. "Yeah, this one feels fine. I'll take it," Cameron said.

The blacksmith nodded and handed Cameron a sword belt. Cameron buckled the sword belt around his waist and stowed the sword. They worked their way over to a rack of knives but Cameron kept catching his sword on all sorts of things, slowing his movement.

The blacksmith had Cameron choose five knives and five different sheaths that could be placed all over his body. One knife went in his boot. Two were attached to his waist. Another was across his chest and the last one was up his sleeve.

"There," the blacksmith said, "I think you are properly outfitted for battle!" Cameron nervously bit his lip to keep his teeth from chattering. The blacksmith patted him on the back and wished him luck but Cameron barely heard it over the pounding of his heart in his ears.

As he was leaving, Cameron felt like he would throw up or faint, so he slowly sat down on a rock outside the armory tent. He'd fought before but it was always one on one and he could focus all his energy on the one person or creature that was attacking him. This was all-out war. There would be more than one person trying to kill him at the same time.

An old beanie with neon colored stripes lay on the rock next to Cameron. He put his hand out just above the hat and whispered an enchantment. He pulled the hat onto his head and tapped it with his knuckles to make sure his magic worked. It was as hard as rock and would make a good helmet.

Before joining the battle, Cameron decided he better practice using his weapons a little. Cameron took out his sword first and tried a few swings but his movements were awkward and stiff so he put it away.

He moved on to his knives. First he started with one knife, commanding it to come out of its sheath and follow his hand movements. He moved his hand side to side and the knife followed. He flipped it and did a stabbing motion. As he added more and more knives with different patterns he eventually had an impenetrable shield of flying knives that would do whatever he commanded.

Cameron was just finishing up when a girl walked up to him. He recognized her as Abigail, one of the girls who had rescued him and Kya near the Taniwha's cavern. She was wearing the same sort of stuff as a lot of the other Canimon soldiers: ammo belt, armor, boots, and a sword on her belt. But one thing completely different was her eyes. When he last saw her she was wearing dark sunglasses, but now he could tell her eyes were completely white. She was blind. He gasped a little as she approached him.

"Hey," she said, "I'm about to head out to the battle with the rest of my unit. Do you want to join us?"

"Uh, sure," Cameron replied, "But I'm not very good. I've never fought in a full-blown battle like this before."

"That's okay," Abigail replied, "You'll do just fine, and we'll be watching your back."

Cameron was befuddled that Abigail could fight without sight. "How," Cameron started, "Do you, um, what happened?"

"How do I fight when I'm blind? Actually, I can see more than anyone else with my other senses. I was born like this. I didn't learn to fight blind, I was just able to do it. My mother was the same way."

Cameron nodded in astonishment. They started toward the battlefield to join Abigail's unit when Abigail heard something and turned her head.

"What is it?" Cameron asked.

"Something... dirty. A troll," Abigail pointed to a small alleyway. At first Cameron didn't see anything but then a shadow flickered between the buildings.

"Let's go!" Abigail yelled as they raced after the troll, following the sounds of it snorting and drooling. After chasing the troll for about five minutes Cameron decided enough was enough and caused a small, square room to rise out of the ground around the troll. From outside, they heard the troll run into the far wall of the room with a thump. To Cameron's surprise, Abigail lifted them off the ground with magic and dropped them into the room with the troll through the open top.

Chapter Sixteen

The troll froze when he saw them, and then tried to bite them, but Cameron tethered the troll to the ground with enchanted rocks.

"How did you get here?" Cameron asked. "We have an army out there fighting you, how did you get past them?"

The troll smiled gruesomely, showing his blackened teeth. "You pitiful humans, thinking you're so special because you can use magic, but compared to us you're nothing. We cannot be stopped!"

"Enough with the chatter," Abigail said and with one swing of her sword the troll was dead. Cameron watched the troll's body slump to the ground and looked up at Abigail.

"This is war," she said. "Show no mercy."

CHAPTER 17

▲ ≋ ⌐ ⌐ ⊬ ■ ✓ ● ♌ ✓ ▲ ▲ ● ⌐

K ya adjusted her breastplate and tugged at her jade bracelet. Emma walked next to her with full body armor and a long sword strapped to her waist. They walked briskly toward the battle that raged around the edges of the camp. Emma insisted that Kya carry a least some kind of weapon so Kya sheathed a small knife in her belt. But her real weapon was the jade bracelet on her wrist.

As they got closer to the battle, more and more people passed them going the other way. Some were wounded but others were just running back with their unit to be rerouted to another area.

"I've got to go," Emma said, "Good luck." She joined a group that was passing them and was gone.

Kya stood in the midst of people rushing back and forth and realized the truth of what was going on.

People were dying, some no older than herself. They would not make it; she was the only hope these people had. They were counting on her to help them. They believed that she was powerful enough to stop Zedoc and his army. Kya looked around her, *All these people; they could be dead by the end of the day. They're all fighting with the hope that I will stop Zedoc once and for all. Can I do it?* Kya's resolve hardened, *I don't care if I can or can't. All these people fight even though it could kill them, so I will do the same.*

Kya jumped off the ground and flew to a position where she could survey the battlefield from above. Most of the Symbari were amassed near the east wall where they were still coming in. The Canimon were attacking the Symbari from all sides, trying to hack their way into the middle of their forces where Zedoc sat on his throne cackling and shooting fireballs from his fingertips.

Kya pulled her arms back, ready to blast a hole into the ground where Zedoc sat but the largest bat she had ever seen smashed into her, clawing at her face and scratching her all over.

They slammed into the ground, banging Kya's head against the hard dirt. Kya rolled on top of the creature and pulled on its energy source. Its pupils shrank and it started shaking while Kya's energy levels increased. Kya stopped and let the creature crawl away whimpering, confident that it wouldn't be able to cause any further harm. As soon as Kya got up off her knees, a big ogre slammed her back to the ground.

Kya's breath rushed out of her lungs and she winced in pain as the ogre kicked her in the side. She rolled away from the ogre and pulled her knife from its sheath. The ogre leaned over her, pulling his fist back, but he was dead before he got a chance to strike.

The body fell away and Cameron pulled his sword out of the ogre's back. He stuck out his hand and Kya took it, sheathing her knife as Cameron pulled her off the ground.

"Good to see you," Kya said. "Oh, and nice hat."

Cameron nodded, "Good to see you too." Then he grinned at her hat comment, "Yeah, we're here to change the world, right? Thought I'd start with the helmets." He turned and blocked a strike from a lizard-man and continued the fight. Kya wondered where

Cameron's sudden fierceness came from. He was usually kind of shy and hated killing anything.

A hand grabbed Kya's hair. It was a troll. Kya spun around and sent a pulse of energy into the troll's gut throwing him against a wall. Another of the bat-like creatures dive bombed her from above, but she grabbed hold of it at the last second and slammed it into the ground. She lifted herself up above the fight again and dropped back down closer to where Zedoc was. Canimon soldiers fell all around her from Zedoc's crazy fireballs.

Kya put a magic shield in front of herself using one of the jewels on her bracelet. She set up rudimentary shields around several other Canimon soldiers too. She blasted her way through the Symbari army, taking out dozens at a time. But it wasn't enough. They just kept coming and coming. It was as if there was no end to them. Even though the battle started hours ago, the attacking soldiers were still flooding through the east wall into the Canimon camp.

Kya was feeling hopeless with no reason to fight anymore. Why should they fight if they're just going to lose anyway?

She swung around and punched a blue orb at one of Zedoc's special assassins who had spotted her. He moved his hand to block it but it just hooked onto his fingers and spread icy tendrils down his arms until he was completely frozen. A second assassin blasted Kya in the back, sending her to the ground. She shot up off the ground and more assassins rose up around her. They shot their own life energy at her and she slowly fell to the ground, screaming with the energy exploding inside her.

All seemed lost. But there was one last hope. And it came when the mountain fought back. Cameron was fighting his way into the Symbari army surrounding Zedoc when the roof of the cavern exploded. He sheathed all his knives so they wouldn't get lost and braced for the impact of all the rock that would surly end his life. But it never came. He looked up and saw a humongous dragon made of rocks swooping down on the Symbari soldiers. There were at least twenty rock dragons, all picking up Symbari soldiers and throwing them across the cavern.

"Yeah!" Cameron screamed, excited now. They could win. They had the dragons on their side. At first the Symbari soldiers scattered in fear but when Zedoc blew one of the dragons out of the sky, they regained their confidence and shot everything they had at the remaining dragons. More and more of the dragons fell to the ground, crushing soldiers of both sides.

Their hope was gone as soon as it had appeared. There were only three rock dragons left and they were circling at the top of the cavern, making weird sounds that could barely be heard over the sounds of the battle. But when the sounds stopped everyone looked up, and then the top of the cavern exploded again with even more force than before.

Kya knew the dragons must really be here this time. She continued to hold off the assassins that had been assigned to take her out, but she had already used up the energy from five of the fifteen beads on her bracelet. Even with the bracelet, it didn't seem she would have enough energy.

Then Kya remembered one of Hemlick's lessons. *If you can't stop it, use it.* She'd never thought of this lesson as very important because if you can't stop something, the fastest thing to do is run away from it. But now she knew what Hemlick meant. She began to open herself up to the energy being thrown at her from the assassins, letting her shield down. At first it felt like it was ripping her apart but then, as she began to use the energy to refill her own energy supply and replenish the beads on her bracelet, it felt good.

Kya began to use the energy against the Symbari. She shot the energy out right as it came in. With magic, when you shoot energy out, you have to open yourself up in order to let it out, so that means other things can come in. Kya used this to her advantage, shooting the energy right back into the core of the assassins when they opened themselves up.

One of the assassins realized what Kya was doing but it was too late. Kya grimaced as the assassin went flying into the air and shattered into a cloud of dust when he hit the ground.

Kya looked up as a large blue leg smashed a hole through the ceiling of the cavern. Most people started screaming, even the rebels because no one was sure which side the monster was on, but once it was clear that the monsters were dragons, the Canimon soldiers knew they were here to help. The Symbari could be defeated!

The Symbari soldiers still fought, pushing the battle further into the cavern as they continued to pour in from the east wall. Dragons flooded through the hole in the ceiling, hundreds of them filling the air and picking off Symbari soldiers.

Kya felt a sense of sadness even though everyone else was rejoicing about the dragons. The dragons meant more of the Symbari dying. Sure, that was good for them but the Symbari were just other magical beings like her fighting for their beliefs even though they were misguided. Kya put her sentiments aside and continued her push into the Symbari army, shooting energy orbs every which way. She caught sight of Cameron with his whirring wall of knife blades. They were both trying to get to Zedoc any way they could.

Kya could also see a group of dragons clustered around the hole the Symbari had made in the east wall and were pouring out of. The dragons were attacking the Symbari troops as soon as they stepped into the Canimon cavern.

Although Kya could not see it, on the other side of the hole the Symbari soldiers had another problem. Zedoc had kept Lone in a cell in Dragon Mountain ever since he removed her from her painting at Kya's estate, and now Lone had escaped. Lone was causing chaos among the Symbari soldiers who were on their way to the battle. They found they had only two choices: be caught up in her jaws like some of their fellow soldiers, or run.

Lone barged through the opening in the east wall, spitting out a Symbari soldier and letting out an earsplitting howl. One of Zedoc's assassins jumped in front of Lone and captured her in a glowing net of energy. He pulled out a glowing whip and smacked Lone on the nose as hard as he could making her yowl and recoil. The rage welled up inside Lone as the whip cracked again and again against her nose.

"Don't do stupid things little kitty," the assassin taunted Lone, "Or I might have to erase your memory again." Lone felt something welling up inside of her. It was some kind of ancient power that was burning to get out. She couldn't hold it in any longer and it burst out in a brilliant flash of light.

Lone fell to the ground and the net around her disintegrated. She got back on her feet, but when she looked around she noticed that she was much taller than before. She turned to the assassin and roared, fire coming out of her mouth. Wait... fire? Lone was in shock. She looked down at her body. Instead of finding her regular fur, she saw scales, wings, and a long spiked tail. *How can this be*, Lone thought, *I'm... I'm a dragon*?! The assassin ran away to get backup and all of the soldiers around Lone froze in fear.

New memories suddenly flooded into Lone's mind. A cave, the army amassed around her, Zedoc, and the assassin who said he erased her memory at one time. Lone started to remember. *Catina, that is my given name*, she thought, *I like the sound of it.*

She saw Cameron amidst the armies and spoke into his mind, *I remember! Zedoc had one of his assassins wipe my memory when I was looking for your father. My name is Catina.* But then more darkened thoughts came back to her. *No*, she thought. *I would never have helped them.*

What? Cameron asked, batting away a sword and stabbing a troll with one of his knives.

Zedoc. I helped Zedoc take over the dragon's home. Just to find your dad. How could I?

Cameron was silent but then he reassured her, *It wasn't your fault. Right now you're fighting for us. Right now is what matters. Make up for what you did. Help us.*

Catina severed the connection and got used to the feeling of her new body by bashing some Symbari warriors into the wall with her tail. She felt kind of awkward and uncoordinated at first but then her movements started to feel natural. The ancient power welled up inside her again and burst out from her in another brilliant flash of light. The other dragons consumed the energy into their power sources and roared in satisfaction. One of the dragons, a pure black one with green eyes, looked at Catina strangely but continued fighting.

Catina located Kya too, and let her in on her new memories telepathically as she took flight into the air as if she had been a dragon all her life. Kya's opinion was a lot like Cameron's, let's not dwell on the past but make up for it now.

Kya thought about Catina's new information as she fought. She ducked a fireball, and right as she popped back up, a dragon whisked her into the sky, its dark blue claws digging into the back of her shirt.

"What are you doing?!" Kya screamed at the dragon. "We're on the same side!" The dragon didn't answer.

Kya was worried. If the dragon decided to let go of her she would fall because she wasn't keeping herself up this time and it would take a few seconds to create her own levitation. Suddenly, the dragon did let go. It flung Kya up into the air and she flipped in circles. Kya screamed and tried to stop her descent but she was too panicked to think. The blue dragon swooped back down under Kya and she landed right on its back. She heard the dragon chuckle in her mind, *And you thought you were going to die.* There was something familiar about that voice...

"Eliza!" Kya screamed, "How dare you!" Eliza chuckled again and swooped upside down to the top of the cavern with Kya hanging on tightly to the scales on Eliza's back. Eliza became serious now and asked Kya what her plan was.

"I'm not sure," Kya admitted. Eliza flew back and forth above all the dragons that swarmed around the battle below.

Well then, Eliza steeled herself, *Here we go.* She turned one last time and then began a dive directly at Zedoc on his throne. Kya realized what Eliza had in mind and pulled herself into a crouch, holding onto a spike on Eliza's back for balance. They got closer and closer to the warlord. At the last moment, Eliza pulled up and Kya jumped from her back, landing right next to Zedoc's throne.

Zedoc immediately turned on Kya and shot a fireball toward her head, but Kya quickly deflected it and shot right back at Zedoc as he dove behind his throne. Zedoc leapt to his feet and shot another fireball at Kya but she deflected it again, this time sending it back at Zedoc's throne. Zedoc shrieked as the fireball hit his thrown and turned it into a blackened piece of charcoal.

"No! My beautiful throne!" Zedoc turned on Kya in anger, "This is your fault. You'll pay!" He threw huge balls of energy at Kya and it was all she could do to keep them away from her. Zedoc was laughing hysterically and increasing the power in his attack. Behind Zedoc Kya saw Cameron with his knives emerge from the army and advance on Zedoc who was preoccupied with Kya. Just as Cameron threw his knives at Zedoc's back, Zedoc turned and stabbed the knives into the ground with a flick of his wrist. He stopped firing on Kya and pulled Cameron toward him.

"Now, now, that's not fair," Zedoc said to Cameron. "You're cheating. That's not how you play." Zedoc kicked Cameron in the stomach and sent him flying into the ground. He turned back to Kya and smiled gruesomely. "Yes indeed, why don't we play fair?" Zedoc swept his hand through the air making a complete circle and everyone fell to the ground asleep, even his own forces. A few low flying dragons fell in an explosion of dirt and rocks.

The silence was eerie. Except for the dragons flying high overhead nothing could be heard. Kya could see the dragons attempting to come down and help her but Zedoc had put up some sort of force field that prevented them from coming down.

The dragons can't come down through the force field, but that doesn't mean we can't go up through it,

216

Kya thought. As Zedoc advanced on Kya, she shot up into the sky, easily penetrating the force field and landing on one of the dragons. Zedoc shot a fireball at the dragon but it swerved out of the way while at the same time Kya jumped to a different dragon soaring in the opposite direction.

"You can't run forever!" Zedoc's insane voice echoed through the cavern. Kya jumped to yet another dragon as Zedoc fired randomly into the air. Now the dragons were doing their best to confuse Zedoc about where Kya was. They were providing landing places for Kya everywhere she jumped and they flew in formations that blocked Zedoc's view. Zedoc's laughing echoed around the cave and Kya began to shoot back at him from her jumps between dragons, making some of her shots curve at him from differing angles. Finally Kya settled on Eliza's back and paused. Zedoc's shooting stopped. That's when she noticed Cameron floating up to the dragons on a column of rock that he had enchanted. As he jumped onto a dragon, Kya caught Cameron's eye and sent him a questioning glance and then he nodded at her.

We need to attack him together, Cameron said in Kya's mind, *I saw a rock about the size of a basketball drop from the ceiling and fall right through the force field, so I think it is designed to stop only large objects from going through. The dragons can't get though, but you and I might be able to.*

Kya nodded, trying to come up with some way for them to get to Zedoc at the exact same time.

Do you trust me? Cameron asked.

Of course.

Then at my signal, we both jump.

What?

Jump. Now. But before either of them could leave their dragons' back, Catina roared and dove toward the shield that Zedoc had put up. Zedoc laughed hysterically, "You can't penetrate the shield from that direction you fool!"

"No!" Cameron screamed at Catina. The shield had seriously injured all of the dragons that had tried to pass through it and Catina was approaching it at a much higher speed than any of the other dragons had attempted. *What is going through her head?* Cameron thought.

218

Even Catina thought she was insane. She hadn't dismissed the injuries the other dragons had experienced by hitting the force field. But she'd overheard Cameron and Kya's telepathic conversation and couldn't bear the thought of Cameron going up against Zedoc when they didn't fully understand the depth of his powers like she did. Somehow Catina knew, deep down inside, that she could get through the force field even though the other dragons couldn't. So she hurtled toward the shield with her wings tucked in tight and her head pointing straight at Zedoc. She hit the shield at full speed but didn't feel any pain. Instead it felt like slipping under the water of a swimming pool. Catina opened her eyes and saw Zedoc's shocked face mirroring her own. She slammed into Zedoc, pinning him to the ground with her claws.

You shall never terrorize again, Catina boldly told Zedoc. She let the ancient energy inside her feed into Zedoc's energy sources. Zedoc's eyes glowed with the energy pouring into him until his body couldn't take it anymore and with a muffled explosion he was reduced to a pile of dust.

The shield above broke and all the warriors in the cavern woke up. The Symbari army scattered as soon as they realized they'd lost. The Canimon soldiers cheered as the dragons circled to the ground and roared in triumph. Kya and Cameron were dropped off near Catina and Eliza changed from dragon form into human form after Kya climbed off her back.

"Are you okay?" Cameron asked Catina.

"Yes," Catina replied, "I wasn't sure I could do it. But I did."

Velkador landed next to the group in a flurry of wind and dirt. "Well done," he said to Catina. He continued looking at Catina like she was another problem he had to solve but not necessarily a bad one, just a complicated one. Velkador addressed Kya, Cameron, and Eliza, "You three need rest. We can take care of the remaining Symbari. Your chaperone is in the Rosemont Hotel. Go there and recover."

Kya knew Velkador was right. She was exhausted. Her limbs felt like lead and her eyelids were heavy. She felt like she would have collapsed on the ground right there if Cameron wasn't supporting her. Three dragons landed around them. Kya, Cameron, and Eliza each

220

climbed on a dragon and they took off for the Rosemont Hotel, becoming invisible as they approached it so humans would not see them. The dragons dropped them off on top of the hotel and they used the fire escape to get into Room 1104. Charles was relieved and thrilled to see them but decided to let them rest before asking them the hundreds of questions he had.

The adventure was finally over for Kya, Cameron, and Eliza and for the first time in days they would get a full night's sleep.

But before any of them could get to bed, Charles' cell phone rang. As soon as he answered it, a bluish-green swirl of patterns burst out from the screen and filled half the room. Everyone jumped into battle-ready stances, Cameron pulling out his knives and Eliza transforming into a Bengal tiger.

Laughter emerged from the patterns as they formed into the shape of a familiar face. "Good to see you still have your wits about you," Hemlick's voice boomed. "I have been following your adventure through my seeing orb."

"And you didn't do anything to help us?!" Eliza yelled incredulously, changing back into a human.

"I found your little enterprise a great opportunity for you to utilize everything I've been teaching you," Hemlick continued. "I never would have allowed any harm to come to you."

"Well, you still should have let us know you were watching us," Cameron said almost as perturbed as Eliza.

"I didn't because that would have given you a sense of invincibility that you would not normally have. This might cause you to behave incorrectly in a similar situation without my oversight. I also had confidence that you could deal with the difficult situations you were faced with."

"How could you be so sure that we would survive against Zedoc?" Kya asked.

"Well, to be honest I wasn't completely sure, but I was very confident. Catina killing Zedoc was a nice surprise, but there's something I failed to mention to you previously. You have all been part of an experiment of mine. The seeing potion that you drink in order to get to my house was infused with energy boosts to increase your life energy. I decided not to tell you before now because I didn't exactly know how much your energy had increased. I'd like to run some tests on that as soon as you get back. As it is, you all performed wonderfully under pressure and I believe I can entrust you with more than I thought. We will advance quickly when you return home. Congratulations on your victory!" Hemlick disappeared, leaving them all a little bewildered and overwhelmed.

"We... were an experiment?" Eliza asked. "I thought we were off limits as guinea pigs for Hemlick."

"I thought so too, before he turned me into a frog," Cameron said.

"When we get back, we need to set up some ground rules on what goes into that seeing potion," Kya said firmly.

"Agreed," said Charles, "Now let's get some sleep."

Nobody complained and everyone headed for bed.

CHAPTER 18

▲ ≈ ⌐ ◆ ⌐ ♍ ✕ ⌐ ▲

K ya stood next to her friends on the edge of the giant cliff on the west facing side of Dragon Mountain. The sun was setting and it was beautiful. Kya's hair blew in the breeze.

"We won," Kya said blankly. "And we're leaving tomorrow."

"I don't want to go," Eliza whined.

"We have to. This is not our home."

"Can't we come on the weekends somehow?" Eliza pried.

"No, we're not going to go to Switzerland every Saturday. The flight is too long," Kya replied.

"But we could use magic," Eliza suggested.

"Perhaps I can arrange this," Velkador said as he walked up next to them. "I am very glad for your help and I wish to repay you."

Eliza was ecstatic, "Make a portal! In our house and here so we can come and go whenever we want!"

"You really don't have to," Kya insisted, but Velkador refused her protest. "It is done, we would be happy to see you anytime."

Kya was glad there would be a portal. The dragons were kind and the rebels here were her friends. Most of them would be going back to their homes across the world but they could always be accessed through the dragons.

Off in the distance to the south Kya could make out a huge group of dragons emerging from the mountain that had been their home for so long. "What are they doing?" Kya asked Velkador. "I thought they already moved back into Dragon Mountain."

"They are moving the Jade Dragon. It holds an extra storage of our energy," Velkador said. They watched as the dragons gently airlifted the Jade Dragon across the valley between the two mountains and landed near them. Catina walked up behind the dragons with a strange glow in her eyes. She was back in her cat form.

"Catina?" Cameron asked.

She didn't answer. The surrounding dragons parted for Catina, remembering that she was the one who won them the war. Catina continued walking towards the statue, slowly changing into her dragon form as she got closer.

Catina touched the nose of the Jade Dragon with the tip of her nose and a wave of energy spread out from the contact.

"You are the secret," Velkador said. "You are what he made for us and hid away."

Catina pulled her nose back and looked at Velkador quizzically, "What do you mean?"

"You were painted, correct?"

"Yes," Catina replied.

"Do you know who your painter was?"

"Ricardo Alvarez Medina Lopez, Cameron's dad." Catina replied matter-of-factly.

"Ah, Ricardo! What a dear, dear friend he was. Many years ago we anticipated that someone might try to conquer us with some kind of deception. Finally, an enchanter came along who we trusted and was strong enough to work with our energy. As a failsafe plan we entrusted Ricardo to store a large quantity of our primordial energy somewhere, in a place that even we did not know. The energy would remain dormant unless it sensed that we were on the verge of imminent destruction. You, Catina, are that energy source."

"What makes you think that?"

"I wasn't sure until now, but I can tell by your connection to the Jade Dragon. Can you feel it?"

"Yes, I feel a kinship to it, like I'm my whole self now. But how does that make me a secret energy source?" Catina asked.

"Ricardo was not just a painter. He was also a sculptor and he made for us the Jade Dragon. He then enchanted it so we could store our energy in it. He must have used the same enchantment to create you. That is why you feel such a connection to the Jade Dragon."

Catina paused and then dropped her head down, "But I don't deserve to stay with you after I helped the Symbari."

"Nonsense," Velkador said, "The Symbari killed Ricardo because they knew your feline instincts would overcome you and drive you to go looking for him and eventually come to them for help. They needed your power to create the virus that sickened us and drove us out of our mountain."

"But how did they know Catina even existed, let alone that she had special powers?" Kya asked.

"Symbari spies are all over the world. There must have been one near Catina's painting that sensed there was something special about her even if they did not know specifically what it was that was so special," Velkador mused.

"The Shadowed Man," Cameron said as Kya nodded her head.

"I am still ultimately responsible for what I did," Catina sadly reasoned.

"Yes," Velkador replied, "But you also ultimately lived up to your responsibility to us and Ricardo. We would not be returned to our rightful home without you and for that we shall consider your slate wiped clean."

"I still feel like I have very little understanding about how this power inside me works," Catina said.

"You should remain in your cat form until we have trained you to handle your dragon power. In your cat form, the dragon energy is dormant; in your dragon form you have so much more power than you can ever imagine." Velkador then turned to Cameron, "You too. The power you inherited from your father remained dormant until you came to know without a doubt that you had it in you. Neither you nor Catina have used even an ounce of your true power."

Cameron's father was a more amazing man than Cameron had ever thought. But then why would he leave his family? When he voiced this question to Velkador a concerned look crossed the dragon's face. "When your father moved the dragon power we gave him and stored it in Catina, traces of it were left on him. Those traces of power were getting him noticed by other creatures and they were coming after him. He didn't want any of his family to get caught in the crossfire of an assassination attempt. Leaving was the only way he could hope to guarantee the safety of you and your mother."

Velkador noticed Cameron's sudden realization that his father left the family not because he wanted to leave them, but because he loved them. Knowing that Cameron, and Cameron alone, had to come to terms with the circumstances surrounding his father's death and decision to leave his family, Velkador quietly left the cliff, escorting the group of dragons with the Jade Dragon back into the center of Dragon Mountain.

Kya, Cameron, Eliza, and Catina all looked out at the sunset with its swirling colors across the horizon. Kya reached for Cameron's hand and he took it. Her other hand grasped Eliza's. Cameron laid his hand on Catina. They had saved the world. They had discovered new strengths. They had gained many new and wonderful friends. They stood together, strong and united, wondering what their next adventure would bring.

About the Author

Kara Winters is a teenager full of life, energy, and imagination. *The Grimalkin's Secret* got its start at the dinner table while Kara and her mom were working on the Word Power challenge found in Reader's Digest. They came upon the word "grimalkin" which means: cat, particularly an old female cat, or a bad-tempered old woman. Kara thought grimalkin was a cool word and when later assigned to write a short novel in school, decided to center her story around it. After school ended, Kara continued adding to her story until it got to its current length. Along the way, Kara's mom, dad, brother, and other members of her extended family offered suggestions for improvement, making this a family sourced book of sorts.

Coincidentally (or not?), in the middle of writing her book, a black and white grimalkin started showing up in Kara's yard. To this day the grimalkin occasionally lounges in a chair on the south-facing front porch. Sometimes, at night, the grimalkin looks through the window in the back door before wandering off on some unknown adventure in the mice-filled field next door.